MY
HUNGRY
FRIEND

Daniel
Barnett

To Janie,
I'm sorry about the spiders.

Thank you, Sadie!

PART ONE
BLACK
TOOTH

1

One kick.

That was all it took.

One kick, and a cup of change.

I squeezed off the train at Harvard Ave, sweating underneath my collared shirt and pea coat, and walked toward the worst mistake of my life. It was a cold, cloudy day, no sight of the sun to be found. In Boston, March isn't a month. It's a proper noun describing the long, gray trudge between winter and spring. Everyone had their heads down and their hands in their pockets, except for the people sitting on the sidewalk. *They* had their heads up and their hands out. I have nothing against the homeless, but when they come out in numbers, they make getting down the block a guilt trip. You help none of them, you feel bad. You help one, and you have to practically run by the rest. There's never enough to go around, and sometimes you're just cashed out. Even if you're carrying around a roll of quarters in your pocket, sometimes you're just cashed out.

That morning there were the usual faces. One was a black fellow in a sleeping bag with big white eyes that seemed to jump out of his head. Another was Napkin Guy, who'd earn enough for a cup of coffee and use the coffee to purchase a few hours of real estate in Dunkin Donuts, making gorgeous, intricate flowers out of paper and straws. There was a woman who never stopped swinging her arms and calling out, "Can I have a dollar? Can I have a dollar? Can I have a dollar?" Occasionally she wore a leg brace, but today she'd left it . . . wherever she left her things. I'm not saying she's a faker, but sometimes I wondered if she wasn't just out to make a buck. Down that little strip of Harvard Ave, I passed maybe six homeless people in all, some parked next to shopping carts of recyclables, one or two holding urgent, anxious conversations with themselves (but still able to give me entreating stares as I went by) and soon I was biting down on the urge to scream, "I'm not a goddamn piggy bank!"

I wish I had screamed, but I didn't. I did something worse.

And it made me feel *good*.

For a moment.

There's a woman on the corner that everyone calls Mom because she calls everyone who passes 'her sweet child.' She'd sat on her corner underneath an old movie theater marquis since Boston was nursing on the Queen. Her voice was melted chocolate and cigarettes and her skin was as thin as parchment paper, so she was forced to hide herself under thick blankets and wear a hood over her lined face. Every winter I expected her to die, and every spring she was still there.

"My sweet child," she said as I rounded her corner. "Can you spare a—"

That was when my foot found her Styrofoam cup in its path, and I could tell you I had no time to change course, that what happened next was an accident, but I won't. I kicked it. Like a boy at an empty soda can, I kicked her cup of change . . .

. . . *and followed through*, swinging my leg up through the hip and nearly spinning myself around in the process.

Quarters, dimes, nickels, pennies—the whole shebang—exploded in every direction. They ran down the sidewalk. They rolled into the intersection. A few even made it to the other side of the street. The sound of them scattering was music, and my outgoing breath stretched itself into something thin and strange in order to escape my throat, which closed tight in excitement. The noise I made was almost a yelp, like *I'd* been kicked. Everything went quiet in my head. I'd shocked my own inner audience into silence.

At long, long last my foot touched back down. I looked at Mom, who looked up at me from her deep hood, her face wide open . . . that is how I remember her in that moment, not hurt or surprised, but *open*, as though I'd knocked down some door inside her and let the wind into her house. All those many, many winters she'd sat there on her corner, and I let the cold in. *I* let the cold in, do you understand?

I hunched my shoulders and strolled away, my whole body desperate to break into a run. My office was one of six tucked out of sight underneath a concrete overhang, but she must have known where I worked and what I did. She had been there a long time, after all. I went into the warmth, blushing and apologizing for being late, and that was how the first day of my last week on Earth began.

2

The name of my practice is "Show Me Your Smile!" and before lunch I repeated this catchphrase to six different children, including one exceptionally unlucky eleven year old who I had to schedule for a root canal. My own smile was hiding somewhere back between my ears, and forcing it out for an appearance made the muscles in my cheeks hurt. I burped almost nonstop—sick, anxious burps that poisoned the air in my mouthmask. When Lucy, my receptionist and dental assistant, offered to pick up Indian food, I declined. Instead I went down Beacon with a fifty dollar bill rolled in one fist, thinking *this will take care of it, this will more than do.* The corner under the marquis was empty except for a few scattered coins. Mom was nowhere to be seen.

"The lady who sits over there," I asked Napkin Guy. "Where is she?"

"Left."

"Where did she go? Do you know?"

He sniffed a lacy white paper rose. Deeply. This was getting me nowhere. I told him I liked his flower, then I went back to the office. For the rest of the day my guilt was like a cavity in the back of my mouth. Until I got it filled in and capped, I wouldn't be able to focus on anything else.

That's why I took the girl in, mostly. Guilt. Not goodwill. Guilt.

I had finished my last appointment and was putting on my coat when Lu poked her head in through the door. "Mike, there's a young lady here hoping to see you."

"Tell her to schedule an appointment."

"I tried to, but she said she's in a lot of pain. I think"—Lu dropped her voice—"I think she's had things pretty rough."

"What do you mean?"

"You know, like on the street. She has money, though. A whole wad of it. She must have saved up a long time to come here."

I glanced at the clock: 4:28. I was already going to be late getting home to relieve Cassie, but I was usually late getting home to relieve Cassie and she never seemed to mind an extra hour or two with my mother—as challenging as those hours could sometimes be. Besides, staying longer would give the old woman extra time to return to her corner, and more than anything I wanted her to be there when I left. I couldn't wait until tomorrow to make things right. I wouldn't get any sleep if I had to take her cup of change to bed with me tonight.

And, yes, there was the suggestion that the girl might be homeless. Would I have said yes otherwise? Would I have invited her in otherwise?

"All right, let's see her."

"Really?"

"Really. Just get her info first if she's got any."

The girl walked in as I was fetching my lab coat back out of the closet. She was tall, slim but not starved, and dressed in yesteryear's clothing: boots with holes in them, blue jeans with ripped knees, and a pullover sweatshirt about five sizes too big. One glance at her face, pulled tight from the ponytail she wore, told me that I'd be pushing if not exceeding the limits of my pediatrics' specialization by seeing her. I'm more than capable of peeking into an adult's mouth, of course, but doing so takes business from the general practitioners and is a great way to lose their referrals.

"Hello, Dr . . ."

"Dr. Roberts," I said. "But you can call me Mike. Everyone else does. And you are?"

She paused briefly. "Tiffany."

"Nice to meet you, Tiffany. What's bothering you?"

Her mouth worked silently, as if she was sucking on one large and painful gumball. "I don't know, but there's something wrong."

"Well, let's have a look." I nodded at the chair while putting on latex gloves. She took an anxious seat. Nobody, except for children too young to know better, gets into that chair looking comfortable. Most treat it like a medieval torture device, and that's pretty much what it is underneath the cushions. "All, right, Tiffany. Show me your smile."

Until then Tiffany hadn't given me more than a glimpse of her teeth and, to tell the truth, I wasn't expecting a pretty sight. The homeless have bigger concerns than dental care. But I was wrong. Her smile was beautiful—straight, clean, and perfectly white. Even pained, it made her face light up.

"Did you have braces?" I asked out of pure reflex.

She shook her head.

"You're lucky then," I said, and winced inwardly, glancing at her worn, baggy clothes. They smelled as if they had been washed in men's body spray, and I guessed that was more likely than a Laundromat. "Okay, Tiffany, open up wide."

She opened up wide, and I leaned over her, not realizing until it was too late that I had forgotten to put on my mask. Thankfully, her breath matched her smile and not her outfit. I smelled peppermint and some faint citrus that might have been lemon or lime. I've got a good nose. My mother used to make me sniff her wine back when I was a kid. I would start off by listing what was there—blackberries, granite, so on— but I'd always finish with something absurd like 'wet teddy bear,' or 'baby pillow.' My mother would laugh, and then . . .

"Dr. Roberts?" said Tiffany. "Do you see anything?"

"Sorry. It's been a long day." I turned my eyes forward to the present. A quick scan of her teeth showed nothing out of sorts. No nasty brown spots, no lesions. "Well, we're not dealing with a cavity. And you're not showing any signs of gingivitis."

Then I saw it. A tiny lump behind the 29th and 30th posteriors—in laymen's terms, the teeth set halfway back on the lower left side of her mouth. The gums there had begun to climb the enamel, and under them something bulged. A supernumerary tooth? Those usually presented themselves in children, but a late erupter wasn't out of the question. This one had probably been camping out down in the roots of her posteriors, and now it was getting ready to show its ugly little head at long last. Strange, though, that her other teeth hadn't been displaced at all. I glanced at Tiffany. Her eyes were watching me closely, with what struck me in that moment as cold interest. For a second I felt as if I were the one in the chair under examination. I looked back into her mouth. Blinked. The lump had risen closer to the surface . . . unless the gums covering it had crept back ever so slightly, and wasn't it odd that those gums weren't swollen or bleeding? I gave them a poke to test their tenderness, but instead of squishing beneath my fingers, they *moved.* No, that is only halfway to the truth. Her gums didn't just move under my touch; they shrank from my touch, sliding down like a clingy red robe. Something pricked me—something that looked like a baby canine tooth but completely black, and I pulled my hand out with a gasp.

Tiffany shut her mouth. She got up out of the chair. "Thank you, Dr. Roberts, for seeing me. I feel so much better now. How much do I owe you?"

I was too bewildered to answer.

"Come on, Doctor, you don't work for charity. Everything's got a price." She thumbed a few bills out of her pocket. "One hundred dollars. That's ten a minute. Does that seem fair?"

"What—what was that?"

"What was what?" she said, smiling a thin bright smile. She dropped the money on the chair. "Goodbye, Doctor, and good luck." At the door she paused and gave me a long, thoughtful look. A look with no warmth in it whatsoever.

"Everything's got a price," she said.

Then she left.

I stood there staring after her until I became aware of the tingling, throbbing heat in my right hand. A drop of blood welled from my forefinger, spreading between my skin and the skin of my glove.

3

The sun was setting, and the clouds simmered reddish purple to the west. To the east, where I was headed, the sky was already dark. I had spent five solid minutes disinfecting the prick on my fingertip, first with rubbing alcohol and then with hot water and soap. Still the tingling continued.

Mom's corner was a shadow underneath the old marquis, but not an empty shadow. A hooded face watched me from a lump of blankets. Those blankets were brown, I know that, but in my mind they're red. Like gums.

"Ma'am?" I said. "I'm sorry for earlier. I hope this helps."

I held out the fifty dollar bill, now wrapped in the hundred dollars that Tiffany had left me. I wanted to be rid of it all. To wipe the day off the slate and start fresh tomorrow.

Mom looked at the money. Then she looked—at least I could swear she did—at the Band-Aid on my index finger. Finally, she looked at me. Her eyes were as dark as the coming night, and terribly sad. "My sweet child," she said. "My poor, sweet child, there is nothing to be done now."

"Just take it. Please."

"What has been given cannot be taken back. By anyone."

"That doesn't make any sense."

"It will."

I pocketed the money, feeling confused and frustrated and tired. Tired, most of all. As I turned to leave, one wrinkled and surprisingly strong hand shot out from her blankets and clamped my wrist. "Mind the cracks," she said. "Watch where you walk and where you reach, and never go any place you can't see into first. Even if it's in your own house."

While she spoke, a bottle fly crawled out of her beaked nose, walked to the cusp of her upper lip, and rubbed its black forelegs together luxuriously. The sight of it held me there. I did not feel her let go, did not realize I was free to move until I was already moving away, and soon I was on the green line bound for home.

4

My mom and dad met at college right here in Boston. He was a business major from a small town in Texas with a lust for cowboy hats that no amount of ridicule could kill. She was city born and a groupie for Karl Marx. They hated each other from the very beginning.

I was born before either managed their Bachelor's degree. To my dad's Christian family, I was something of a bastard; being born out of wedlock made me a permanent blind spot to them. I've gotten a few Christmas and birthday cards from their clan over the years, but I've never seen their faces outside of photographs. My mom's side didn't care much for the coupling, either. Her parents were devoutly liberal and atheist, and I'm pretty sure they looked at my fetus as some sort of prenatal hijacker, as if my mother's body were a vehicle that I had taken control of violently with the intent of driving her toward a life of obligation and unfulfillment. Nothing she said could convince them that my dad wasn't forcing her to keep me. They eventually wrote her a check to have 'it taken care of.' My mom deposited the check and put the money toward an apartment in Cambridge. Her parents didn't speak to her again until she released her memoir four years later (most of this I learned from reading that same memoir, which enjoyed top placement on Ivory Tower bookshelves as well as a darling of a review from The New Yorker). They were proud, they said, 'to have helped shape her literary development.' They bought me a Moleskine notebook in the hopes I might follow in her footsteps, which to them were *their* footsteps, and being four at the time I used the blank pages for some exemplary doodles that my mother tacked to the refrigerator. I haven't tapped into my creative side once in the three decades since. Unless you count what you're reading now. But I'm not writing this for fun. I'm writing this to stay sane.

Dad got his first real paycheck for something related to home security systems when I was six. He and my mother bought a house in Savin Hill, a cute seaside community in Dorchester that earned the colorful nickname Stab 'N Kill for no apparent reason other than it was catchy. We moved out of the one bedroom, and on our first night in our new home, my dad did the cheesiest thing of his short and unsentimental life. He bought a diamond ring, tied the ring to my head using my hair, and sent me to my mother wearing one of his cowboy hats, knowing she could not stand the sight of me taking after his filthy western ways. She plucked off the hat as expected and turned about ten years younger in one wonderful moment that I will never forget. I may never have had the chance to really get to know my dad, but he made me a part of making my mother happier than I have ever seen anyone since, and that counts for a lot, I guess. One month before their wedding he went down to the basement in the middle of the night to fetch some logs for the fire, and a bad circuit blew in his brain. My mom woke up as their bed cooled, and she spent nearly half an hour wandering the dark house before she found him dead by the woodpile. She saw a few men after that (and a woman or two, I suspect), but nothing serious ever came out of the affairs. In her heart she was still engaged to my father.

Coming back from work under winter's early sunset, I walked through the noise of the overpass into the sudden and always alarming quiet of Savin Hill. Swings dangled limp in the empty playground. Waves lapped gently near the boardwalk where I used to skateboard (and before that, to my great shame, scooter). Sleepy Victorians looked over the street, each one a slightly different color than the last. Since I was a kid, the houses in this community have reminded me of people—all unique but essentially the same. I miss them now. I wish I could see them, but they are not there anymore.

My mother's home is one of the few that was built with space to breathe. It has a backyard with trees and a vegetable garden, a picket fence, and a paved comma of driveway that separates the front lawn into tidy green portions she named Clause One and Clause Two. At least, it used to have all these things, and that evening I walked up the cobblestones to the front door not knowing what a privilege it was to be able to do that.

I knocked. My house key dangled on a chain around my neck, and I did not have the motivation to take it off. Also, I'm right handed, and my right hand wasn't feeling too hot. Or more accurately it was feeling *too* hot. The index finger had begun to swell, filling its sleeve of the glove like a sausage cooked inside the casing. I didn't want to bend it, and I didn't want to think about it either.

Fast, purposeful footsteps moved through the house, and I heard the rattle of Cassie's key. Both the front and back door have double-keyed locks out of necessity. My mother had wandered outside once and walked almost all the way to Milton on the trails that run by Quincy Bay. Two high school kids saw her strolling in her slippers and nightgown, called the cops, and shared their cigarettes with her to pass the time. Thank God it had been July and comfortable out, not January.

Cassie opened the door, and I had to fight the urge to take a step back, as I always do when I see her. It's not that she's beautiful, which she is, or that I'm in love with her, which has been the case since I interviewed her for the job last spring in a coffee shop by the Common. It's that she's big. I don't mean heavy. I mean big as in she fills up wherever she is whenever she's there, and that goes especially for the house where we live together happily, even now, in the place I've built for us inside me. Her skin is dark, but she is bright, my Cassie—she makes me want to write bad poetry about candle flames that go on burning in the rain or wind.

"Hi Mike," she said, stepping back to let me inside. I both worried and hoped that I would brush her, and when I didn't, I felt disappointed as well as relieved. She was wearing black jeans and a faded blue chambray shirt that I wanted to lay my head on as I fell asleep. Ripping it off wouldn't have been so bad either, as long as we're on the subject of conflicting emotions.

"Sorry I'm late. How is she?"

"She's a lovely old gal, and right now she's taking a lovely old nap." Cassie gave me a look that was like a touch on the shoulder. "How are you?"

"I'm okay."

"Then take off that raincloud you're wearing. It doesn't look good on you." She gave me a real touch now, a thump on the back. "Show. Me. Your. Smile."

I thought of the girl in the dentist chair, of the tiny lump hiding behind her perfect front teeth, and managed to move one corner of my lips.

"Better. But not much." Cassie crossed her arms. On most people the gesture closes them off, but Cassie wears it at an ironic, amused angle, as if she's holding onto a good joke. "You know what you need? You need to draw yourself a nice motherfucking bubble bath, and never mind that you're a big strong boy. I'm serious. Go do it now, and don't come out until you're pruned. I'll stick around. I won't even charge you extra."

"I already owe you extra," I said, remembering the bills in my pocket. I peeled off my gloves and thumbed a few out blind. "Here."

"You think I'm going to take that, you're a fool. Good lord, get yourself a cab once in a while."

"But—"

"None of that. I know why you're still riding the train, and it's not because you like the company."

She was right. Cassie Llynch might have been five years younger than me at thirty-four, but she had an MS in nursing with a background in degenerative brain disease that made my own specialization resemble a high school diploma. To live up to her salary, I'd been forced to cut a few conveniences from my life.

I lowered my hand. She grabbed it. "What in the hell happened to your finger?"

The skin around the Band-Aid was puffy and red, and the nail looked as if it had gotten caught in a car door.

"Nicked it," I said. Then I added, "The other day."

"You'd better get it checked. That looks ugly."

"I will tomorrow if it's not better."

"Promise?"

"Yeah. I'll reschedule a few afternoon appointments if I have to." I wasn't lying to make her feel better. If given the choice right then I'd have taken a penicillin shot to the heart, only I was worried what I really needed was anti-venom.

Infections didn't set in this fast, and that tooth . . . that black tooth . . . it had looked almost like a fang.

Cassie was still holding onto my hand, but no longer looking at it. "I wasn't joking earlier, Mike," she said, staring right at me. "You need to give yourself a break. Take a night off. You'll wear yourself down if you don't, and you'll do no good for anyone then. Not her, and not you. Tomorrow I've got my class to teach, but the day after tomorrow, I'm free all night. You say the word, and I'm here with Chinese and a pair of earplugs. You'll go to bed fat, I promise you, and you won't have to get up again all night."

"That's really sweet, Cassie. I'll think about it."

She let go of my hand at last, and still far too soon, and patted me on the cheek. "It's nothing to think about. Don't be a dumb man, Mike. Nobody's got time for that. Especially you."

"All right," I said finally. "Wednesday."

Cassie kissed me on the cheek, something she had done once or twice before, but never so softly. "Good boy."

5

The living room reappeared after Cassie left. It had always been there of course, but I had not been able to see it past her. I found myself standing in a quiet house with dark purple carpeting, dark brown walls, tall oak bookcases, and leather everything else. I locked the door and then put the chain with the key back around my neck. Cassie wore her own key the same way for easy access. Fires are a danger in any home, but they become a real worry in households where a family member has a habit of absentmindedly turning on the burners over the stove. Particularly when all exits are locked.

A Tupperware of chicken salad waited in the refrigerator. Cooking for me as well as my mother wasn't a part of Cassie's job description, but she always made a little extra, and I was more than thankful for that today, having fed myself nothing but anxiety since breakfast. I scooped some into a bowl and ate as I walked upstairs, using my less-practiced left hand to hold the fork because of my bad finger. My mother's room was dark. I peeked in on her to see if she was showing any signs of waking. She wasn't, and I was thankful for that too. I needed—

Just thinking the word, *needed,* unlocked a door inside me.

I needed a shave (my mustache hairs were poking me in the lips, and my beard was beginning to adventure down one side of my neck). I needed a shower. I needed a bubble bath and a six pack of beer to go along with it—and maybe a dream or two of Cassie. I needed music. Loud music. I needed a hard run, a good scream, a long night's sleep. But what I needed most of all was in the room down the hall, where I now sit, typing this.

My mother's office was not much bigger than my freshman dorm room, which I could clear in one hop. There was a single window curtained by plush blackout drapes. There was a closet so tiny it was almost nonsensical, tucked in the back where the ceiling sloped down and hidden behind a half-sized door. And there was a desk of polished hardwood on which sat an ancient IBM typewriter. Its E and T keys had been worn blank from use, and the space bar rested at a crooked angle from being struck always on the left side, by my mother's left thumb. A fresh sheet had been loaded into the carriage for tomorrow. This was a part of her ritual, the new page waiting in its place. When I was a kid, I never needed an alarm clock. No morning went by when I did not wake to the sound of her clacking away in here. Over her career Bev Jacoby wrote and published eight acclaimed but decidedly unpopular novels, four collections of poems, and two self-memoirs, the first recounting her bohemian childhood and extradition from that world into the role of a young mother. The second, titled *My Hungry Friend*, came shortly after her diagnosis and charted her first creeping footsteps into the alien landscape of Alzheimer's. The book was billed as "honest and heartbreaking" by The New York Times, and while it may have been those things on the surface, it was horror underneath the skin, the work of someone haunted—hunted—and holding on white knuckled to herself. At first my mother's hungry friend is a jokester. It eats the sofa in the living room and replaces it with a stranger's couch. It picks the car keys right out of her hand and leaves her walking around the house looking for them. Then it begins to take bigger bites. It swallows the backyard and spits up a forest that she becomes lost in while searching for her carrot patch. It munches away the route to the grocery store, the art house movie theater, the river, turning the city where she has lived her whole life into a concrete jungle roamed by roaring metal beasts and bug people who move about in herky-jerky packs. By the final chapter the faces of her friends, her son, have been licked clean of all familiar features. The closing lines of the book I'll never forget, for they terrified me.

"My hungry friend follows me where I go. He takes a nibble here, a nibble there, and where I am I do not know."

It wasn't just what was said in those final words. It was the slight erosion of her careful syntax and the presence of that almost sing-song rhyme. Some piece of architecture in her head had begun to slip. The room that contained her prose became the next meal for her hungry friend, and before the book hit shelves, she was no longer able to construct meaningful sentences. She turned to poems, and that did her well for a while. Very well. She wrote free verse with more success than she'd ever had. Her final collection won The National Book Award for poetry, though she could not quite understand what that meant by the time the results were announced. I moved out of my Allston apartment and back into the house shortly thereafter. My girlfriend at the time was upset by my decision. She wanted me to send my mother to a home, but she did not know my mother's ritual. She did not know that my mother's most lucid hours of the day were the sunrise hours spent in her office at her typewriter. In the shrinking house that was my mother's brain, poetry was her last and brightest room.

At least, it had been.

I sat down at her desk as I had done that morning before work. This was not something I did frequently, but the night had been a bad one for Bev Jacoby, meaning it had been a bad one for me too, and I had needed (there was that word again) something to pass the time until daybreak. So I'd made some coffee and come into her office to do a little reading. Thinking, I don't know, thinking I'd catch up with her. Or maybe I'd known then. Maybe I'd known for a while, and that was why I hadn't ventured in here in months. I opened the top drawer where she kept her poems, took out one of her latest works, and began to read—just as I was doing now. Unlike that morning, however, I did not shove the poem back into the drawer after the first few lines.

Sonlight on the walls
Sonlight falls
The halls go
dark
Hello?

I was warm
I am cold
cracked
An eggshell
that drips

Put me together
I am apart

Make me

hole

When I finished, I read it again standing it up. I read it a third and fourth time, pacing slowly around the room. At last, I leaned my forehead on the downslope of the ceiling and let my knees go limp, so that my neck took on the weight of my body. I stood there like that until the muscles along my spine and shoulder blades began to ache. I was as close to laughing as a person can be without laughing. I sounded like an overheated dog.

I crumpled the poem into a ball and threw it into the corner, where the ceiling was lowest. I could still see the poem, though, and I needed, needed, *needed*, not to see it. Almost falling over in my hurry, I bent over to grab it. I ripped open the office's tiny closet, tossed the poem inside, and slammed the door. Then I put my back to the door and sat there with my face in my hands. That morning I had taken a glimpse of the poem, a nibble, if you will, and made myself stop before it got all the way inside me. I'd gone through the whole day like someone with a lump of spoiled food caught in the throat, trying desperately not to swallow. But I'd swallowed now, all right. I'd eaten my fill, and nothing could stop what came next.

I sobbed, and while I sobbed, I banged my head back against the closet door. Knock. Knock. Knock. I must have been making a good deal of noise because soon came an answer.

"Who's there?" my mom called, from out in the hall.

I stopped everything, breathing too, and stared at the office door in a state that was close to terror. I did not want to see her. Or be seen by her.

"Who is it?" My mother's footsteps moved downstairs. She was going to the front door, I realized. Once there, she'd try to answer it, and would go on trying, getting more and more frustrated because the door was locked. I heard the knob click, and click, and click. "Who's there? Who's there?"

My face was sticky wet, and so were my hands. Snot hung in ropes from my nose. I wiped them away with my sleeve, started to get up, and looked back at the closet. Leaving my mother's poem in there seemed wrong, whether or not she would ever realize it was gone. Leaving her poem in there would be like . . .

Coins scattering down a sidewalk.

Like that.

The office had only two light bulbs, both over the desk, and their glow did not reach inside the closet. I felt around for the poem in the dark. There are two other things I need to make clear before I go any further. The first is that I wasn't paying any attention to what I was doing. My head was already onto what I'd do next—uncrinkle the poem, stick it back in the desk, and go separate my mother from the front door. The second thing is that the office resides just below the house's pitched roof, which is why the ceiling slopes down on one side of the room and why the closet is no more than two feet tall . . . and deep. On the other side of its back wall, there's insulation followed by gray shingles and the great outside.

I pawed around for the crumpled ball, and when my fingers did not find it, I crawled into the closet a bit. Still no poem. I crawled in some more. Now I was in up to my shoulders, and my mother's voice (*"who's there . . . who's there?"*) sounded very far off. Worlds away. A moment later I could not hear her at all. The carpet under me was soft, much softer than the carpet in the office, and did it feel damp? Or was that the slobber and tears on my hands? I crawled deeper, and that was when I remembered the closets in our house all had bare floors. Every one of them. Moisture began to soak through the knees of my slacks. I looked back over my shoulders.

Only my feet were still in the office.

The rest of me was in the closet.

My hands clenched, and my fingernails dug into what I'd thought was wet carpet, what I wanted so badly to be wet carpet . . . but if it was carpet, then why were there no threads? Why were there no *threads*? My head turned forward slowly in the dark. A warm, humid draft touched my face. The smell was low and salty and spoiled, like a harbor full of shored fish. On the coattails of the draft came a whicker. Soft but big. The sound gave shape to the space around me, the space that was no longer a closet but something— some*where*—else.

A powerful shudder ran through my body, as if a cold taut wire inside me had been sharply plucked, and I came unfrozen. I backed into the office, tipped onto my behind, and kicked the closet shut. I kept kicking until I had shoved myself all the way across the room and into the desk, making the keys rattle in my mother's typewriter.

Downstairs the doorknob clicked, clicked, clicked.

"Who's there . . . who's there . . . who's there?"

6

I'd had a long day. I'd been in a heightened emotional state. The closet was the size it had always been, which just happened to be not quite as itty-bitty as I'd originally thought. It wasn't as if I spent much time poking around in the damn thing, and maybe there *was* carpet or a rug of some kind in there, not to mention a serious breach in the woodwork for there to be such a bad draft and so much damp. Never mind that March had barely dripped . . . February had rained and snowed enough for two winters, and so what if I hadn't been able to find my mother's poem? I'd look for it tomorrow. Yeah. Tomorrow. Or maybe on the weekend.

This was the conversation I was having with myself as I went about the next hour. After that I wasn't thinking of the closet at all. I'd gotten good at not thinking about unpleasant things. Not thinking, for me, was a well-developed muscle. I put it to practice every time I changed my mother's diaper or gave her a bath or replaced her soiled sheets at two in the morning. You don't turn your brain off because it's the easier way. You turn your brain off because it's the only way. You close your eyes and you keep walking, because blind is the best you've got.

I ate my dinner. I brushed my teeth. I washed my hands because they stank like saltwater, like bad fish. I did not stop to think about where that stink had come from, even though it was in my slacks, too. I did a load of laundry. I took a shower, not a bath, because a bath required laying down. If I let myself lay down, I would fall asleep, and there was so much to be done. There was always so much to be done.

7

Around one in the morning, I woke to a voice calling my father's name throughout the house.

"John . . . John . . . John?"

My head was groggy, and my right hand felt strange, lopsided, as if all the blood in it had gone to the forefinger. I tried to close that finger, but it was swollen straight. Bending it even a tiny bit sent a chilling tingle up the back of my arm. I went downstairs. A hazy orange glow was coming from the kitchen. All four burners on the range had been turned on high. I shut them off. My mother always managed to light the flames, but I kept the kitchen window open a crack for gas to get out, just in case.

"John?"

Footsteps padded past the wall that joined the kitchen and living room. A door creaked open. The footsteps moved down and away, growing softer. I followed them to the threshold of the basement. It was dark down there, and to change that I'd have to pull the string over the bottom step. I felt a trill of sleepy, dreamlike unease. *Watch where you walk and where you reach, and never go any place you can't see into first* . . . someone had said that to me, or maybe I had read it somewhere. In one of my mom's books, perhaps.

I went downstairs. I reached for the string and nearly pulled back from the sudden awful fear that I would feel something else hanging there upside down. Drooling lips and a set of cracked and crooked teeth. Oh, the things that visit a dentist's mind in the dark.

I pulled the string.

Light flickered.

My mother stepped around the log pile into view. The stack was no more than five feet tall, but her illness had bent her back, shortened her. She wore a gray nightgown that showed two small, droopy breasts and the bundle of her diaper. Her bare feet picked up the dust on the concrete floor, and not for the first time I wondered at her ability to navigate the dark down here without falling over or bumping into anything. She was lost everywhere she went, and yet some part of her still knew the way.

She turned. Her face was like crumpled paper, like the poem I'd balled up and thrown away. Her eyes widened at the sight of me, and the wrinkles on her forehead temporarily smoothed themselves out. "John!" she said, shuffling my direction with outstretched arms. "There you are. I woke up, and the bed was cold. Goodness, I've been looking for you everywhere."

I let her take my hand and lead me up to her bedroom. When she tried to climb under the covers, I held her ankles and wiped the dust off her feet.

"Goodness it's late. You must be so tired, John."

"Yes," I said, turning off the lights. I got into bed with her and stayed there until she fell asleep, then I went back to my own room.

This was a game we played every night, often twice, sometimes more.

8

I dreamed my forefinger grew longer and redder until it dragged along the floor when I walked. Wherever it touched, a crack appeared. Soon there were so many cracks things began to fall through them. Chairs, couches, the kitchen table, then whole rooms, whole houses and the streets they stood along, until Savin Hill was gone and I was left alone in a strange world.

9

When my alarm kicked me out of bed, I felt a moment of exquisite relief that I could not stand up straight and touch the floor at the same time. The relief quickly faded after I turned on the light and discovered my forefinger was twice as fat as normal. Its middle knuckle reminded me vaguely of Rocky Balboa's squinting eye during his first bout with Apollo Creed (you've gotta cut me, Mick). The soft pink flesh under the nail had taken on a purplish cast, and on the pad of the fingertip, where I had been pricked by . . . whatever I had been pricked by inside that homeless woman's mouth . . . there was a tiny raised lump, like a single dot of Braille.

I might have explained my way through my experience in the office closet, but there was no talking my way through this. Dread planted a black seed in my stomach. I tried to brew a pot of coffee, but I had forgotten where to place the filter, how to pour the water.

"All right," I said. "All right."

I called Lu, my receptionist, and told her to reschedule all appointments for the day because I was sick. This was something I could not, strictly speaking, afford to do, and because Lu worked for an hourly wage it didn't help her either. But she was kind enough to wish me well at the doctor's. I thanked her, and just as I was about to hang up, I said, "Hey, Lu. That woman who came in last minute, Tiffany, did she end up leaving information with you? A last name, maybe?"

"No last name, I don't think." She hmmm-ed. "I think she left a phone number, though."

"Text it to me. When you get into the office."

"Sure, Mike. Can I ask why?"

"She overpaid," I said after a moment.

My mom wandered into the kitchen. The night sky was beginning to pale to the east, which meant I had but a few minutes before the typewriter called her up to the office. I sat her down at the table, turned off the burners that she had already managed to turn on, and rattled out her daily meds and vitamins. There were six pills in all, and she swallowed each of them separately, complaining about every single one. "I don't like it, John. This is yucky, John. This hurts my tummy, John."

I gave her a bowl of oatmeal with plenty of brown sugar mixed in, which was the only way she'd have it. "Here. Get something in you or your stomach will really hurt."

"I wish you made eggs."

"And I wish you'd climbed down from your ivory tower at least once in your life to write a book that actual fucking people would buy. Your last royalty check couldn't fill a coffee cup." I thought of Mom, the other Mom on her street corner, and immediately regretted my choice of words.

"I want coffee."

"You can't have coffee. Your doctor said." I put her spoon in her hand. "Eat your oatmeal."

"I want eggs."

I promised her a dozen scrambled eggs, an entire Starbucks, and Hugh Jackman naked on a platter—if she would just eat her goddamn oatmeal. She ate one bite, spit the bite back into her bowl, and asked for bacon. I went out on the porch and smoked a cigarette in the cold, sea-sharpened air off Quincy Bay.

10

Cassie was glad I'd taken the morning to have my finger checked. She suggested I upgrade my personal day into a bona fide 'me' day after I got spruced up at the doctor's office. "See a movie. Eat a steak." I told her I was planning to snort some blow. She asked me to save some for her. I said I'd try.

I took a cab to urgent care, but only because she called me the cab while I was upstairs brushing my teeth. Tricky, tricky woman. The waiting room swallowed an hour of my time, which was fine by me because I managed to doze through most of it.

My doctor was a balding, bespectacled Chinese man who spoke his way through the English language like someone navigating a dense thicket. I told him I'd nicked myself in a patient's mouth but left out the exact details, not sure if he would believe them or if I truly believed them myself. He took one look at my finger and whistled.

"You should come in sooner, Mr. Roberts. When did this happen?"

"Yesterday."

"You lie. Or you forget." He turned my finger over and eyed the welt. "Are you sure this was not a snake's mouth you reached inside?"

I wasn't sure of that. Not at all. "Just some girl," I said. "But she, well, I'm pretty sure she lives on the street. Maybe she's got something weird, you know."

The doctor nodded as if in agreement, but his eyes were uncertain. He prescribed me a whopping dose of Cephalexin and told me to come back if my finger stayed the same or got any worse. He also suggested I use my 'tooth tools' from now on instead of sticking my bare hands in people's business, and I thanked him for the advice as politely as I could. Condescension is hard to swallow when you've got a finger like a bloated tampon.

I filled my prescription and strolled south through Beacon Hill to the Boston Common, where I got a bagel to protect my stomach from the antibiotics. The coffee shop was hot and crowded, so I took my food outside to the park. March's clouded sky had broken in places, and sunlight shone brilliantly through the cracks.

Sonlight on the walls, I thought. I remembered I had turned my phone off at the hospital and switched it back on in case Cassie had tried to reach me. She hadn't, but Lucy had sent me a text with Tiffany's number. It wasn't strange the girl had a phone; I'd seen more than a few homeless folks carrying around last-generation cells. Hell, I'd seen several rocking smartphones. Besides, she'd had cash. Maybe she worked a corner, or maybe I'd made a poor snap judgment based on her clothes and the fact she didn't use a credit card. The only thing I was certain about was that I had absolutely no idea what I wanted to say to her. *Hi, my finger hurts. Did you happen to poison it with your snaggletooth?*

A dog came limping down the path in front of my bench. It was a golden retriever. It was also a walking billboard for cancer. Its fur was falling out in tawny brown clumps, and its ribs showed through the patches. Skin tags decorated its graying muzzle. It looked happy enough, though. There was a tennis ball in its mouth and a casual wag to its tail. As it got close, a boy of nine or ten intercepted it. He jogged off the field and dropped to his knees so that he and the dog were nose to nose, staring right into each other's eyes. Love at first sight. I was letting the two of them fade into the background when the golden dropped its ball.

Maggots spilled out of its mouth as if from an uncorked bottle. They poured to the ground in a white, writhing stream. More squirmed around the dog's yellowed canines and in the black of its gums. The boy laughed in delight. He scratched the dog's ears and rubbed its jowls. He let the dog lick his face, pinching his lips shut against its crawling white-pink tongue.

All of this I watched from my bench a few feet away. My left hand had clenched around my coffee cup, crushing it. Steaming hot dark roast dribbled over my fingers. I did not notice. Nor did I see the lady coming down the path with a leash bundled in one loose fist until she stopped by the dog.

"You make a friend, Charlie?" she said, and the golden wagged its tail. "Charlie *loves* new friends, doesn't he?"

"How old is he?" said the kid.

"Oh he's getting up there, but he tries not to let it slow him down much." The woman smiled, but her voice held a note of sadness. A maggot plopped onto the toe of her running shoe. The ground around her and the boy roiled with grubby white bodies. "I've got to take him off now, but he'll be back tomorrow same time if you want to say hi."

"Okay," the boy said. He picked up the tennis ball, and a maggot clinging onto the nap popped like a spoiled grape under his thumb. "Here you go, Charlie."

The golden took the ball gently before limping off after the woman. I watched them go, my spilled coffee cooling on my hand. I had not blinked for a full minute. My last bite of food sat dead in my mouth, and suddenly that bite did not feel quite so dead. I spat it out onto my lap, certain I would see something squirming inside it, but there was only chewed bagel and cream cheese.

"Gross, mister," said the boy kneeling in maggots. "*Yuck.*"

11

My mother used to say that if I lost a foot halfway to the store, I'd hop the rest of the way there, buy my groceries, and hop back home before giving my missing foot a second thought. She said I had a 'steadfast mind,' and that nobody with a compass had ever stayed a truer course than me. I don't know if that's true, but after the incident with Charlie and Friend, I found a drinking fountain to wash down my antibiotics. My stomach felt like a bowl of fruit that had gone bad and become a feast for flies, but I took my medicine anyway. Because that was the next step. That was what came after the bagel. What came following that, though, I had no idea. Cassie had suggested I take a 'me' day and see a movie, and right then a dark place where I could turn myself off for a while sounded like a good idea. I walked to the AMC on the Common, bought a ticket for the loudest offering, and for the next two hours I listened to explosions and gunshots and didn't think a single thought. When the credits began to roll, I stayed in my seat.

I was losing my mind.

There it was.

Over the course of three and a half years, I had watched my mother's herselfness drip out of her like water through a sieve, so I was familiar with the process. The fact that it was now happening to me was worrisome. I tried but could not attach any other emotion to it than that. I was still attempting to fit my mouth around the idea, I think; things like this can't be swallowed all at once. They have to be nibbled down and digested bit by bit. What I knew was this: losing my mind would make work harder and eventually impossible. Then I would not be able to pay Cassie. Then I would not be able to support my mother. Finally, I would not be able to take care of myself. The timeline could be short, long, or anywhere in between. There was also the possibility of drugs to slow down the disease's progress, not that drugs had helped my mother much, but insanity came in many different flavors and perhaps there would be something out there to treat my own special brand. There was even the possibility if I allowed myself the hope, and oh how I wanted to, that my episode in the Common had been a one-off, a false alarm brought on by stress and an overworked, under-rested brain. Hell, I'd done LSD in college, and people always talked about acid flashbacks. As long as nothing else happened, I didn't have to worry. I didn't have to worry.

The theater was empty and had been for a while, but the lights hadn't come back on yet. That was strange, considering these places usually brightened after the film ended. Far stranger was that I could no longer see the movie screen. At all. I looked up from my seat in the back row. Light shined ghostly white through the small window above my head. The projector was still running, which meant that the credits should have been rolling as well. I looked back down. My heart began to pound. The bottom few rows were gone. Where the backs of the chairs had been, there was nothing, not even an outline. The aisles ended at the same point, and so did the walls and ceiling. The last visible steps glowed a faint orange, their edges delineated by lightstrips. Those edges might have belonged to a cliff. It was as if the whole front of the theater had fallen into a pit, and now, past the *new* front of the theater, something was coming into focus. Something as large as the figures that had not so long ago occupied the screen. The projector's beam traced an immense shape with outstretched arms. Arms like those on a crucifix, spanning the gloom.

My heart had crawled up into my mouth and was hammering on the wall of my clenched teeth. My hands gripped the armrest. I swallowed, and my spit was thick, gruelly. I felt as if I were tasting my brain run down the back of my throat in a soup.

One of the crucifix's wide arms creaked, bending under some unseen weight. Around its body—its trunk?—there was movement. Slow, sinuous, *unwinding* movement. The projector shut off, and from the dark came a sound like plaque being scraped off an enormous tooth . . . or leathery scales rubbing against smooth bark.

I got up and made for the door in the back (that there was a door there, at the top of the aisle, filled me with a gratitude I cannot adequately express). My shoes stuck against the sticky floor, and hearing that familiar sound alongside the sound coming from below undid my sense of place in the world. It unmoored me.

I stumbled out into the hall and narrowly avoided the garbage can that a clerk was pushing toward the theater.

"Whoa," he said. He caught the door, groaned in annoyance, and mumbled into his walkie-talkie. "Will somebody hit the lights in seven? They're bitching up again." As I walked the other way, I heard him go inside. I did not hear anything else from him—no shout, no scream—and I didn't know whether to be relieved by that or terrified.

12

Crazy. Yes, yes. Crazy. Five minutes earlier, I had just managed to admit the possibility. Now I was uttering it to myself like a prayer. "I'm going crazy. I'm going crazy. I'm going . . . going . . . gone! Home run. Right over the Green Monstah." I started to hum Sweet Caroline, the national anthem of Fenway Park, and then I remembered I didn't like baseball. Much less Neil Diamond. I giggled. Oh boy, oh boy, I was having a me-day now. I fidgeted in place on the escalator as it carried me down to the ground floor. Windows looked out on the tall trees standing in the park, and something about them—their height, the outstretched arms of their branches—made me shiver. I would never come back here. I knew that then. The Common and especially the AMC by the Common were black scribbles on my mental map of Boston. They had been crossed out. They did not exist. Every day that I took the train into work, I would pass under the park and feel it above my head like an enormous black room, an empty theater where maggots wriggled on the floor and unseen things slithered between the seats.

For the rest of the day, I kept moving. Bad things happened whenever I stopped, so I would not stop. I walked from the Common to the brownstones along Commonwealth Avenue. I had lived in this part of the city as a college student, and I ached at the memory of those caffeine-laced days and pot-smoky nights. I took a bridge onto the Esplinade and walked along the river until the cracked sky dimmed overhead and the clouds blushed an alien violet. I walked further than I had ever gone. I walked until I did not know where I was.

13

That night, Tuesday night, was quiet. It was also—and in many ways, still remains—the most horrible night of my life.

I got home after sunset from my wanders west along the Charles. Cassie ran out of the house before my cab could come to a full stop. She was wearing a pencil skirt that stopped just shy of sheer torture—somewhere north of mid-thigh but south of God Have Mercy—and carrying the laptop case she took with her to the community college in Worcester, where she taught a weekly course on degenerative brain disease. I was late. Not so late, however, that she didn't have time to scold me for appearing so haggard.

"You have a full day off, and still you look like you spent all of it on your feet. Epsom salts, Mike. Epsom salts and hot, soapy water. I'd better see you in the morning and not recognize you from a raisin."

She was gone too soon. That's how you tell someone matters to you. They're always gone too soon.

I passed an empty hour in front of the television, feeling like the static that blocked out most of the channels. My mother never believed in T.V. while healthy. She had, quite literally, refused to acknowledge its existence, and I hadn't bothered to have cable installed after moving into the house. Usually I read books, but tonight I could barely tell the print apart from the white space between the lines. When she woke up from her evening nap, I fed her, brushed her teeth, and sent her back to bed. She didn't stay there, though, and by the fifth time I rounded her up, I wanted to grab her by the ears, put my face right in front of her face, and scream, "Go to fucking *sleep!*" If there had been a spare lock lying around the house, I would have happily drilled it into her bedroom door and shut her inside, never mind how I would feel about it in the morning or what Cassie would say. This was the same reason I didn't own headphones: I would use them. I would put them on and pretend my mother into outer space.

Well, lock or no lock, she didn't come out a sixth time. Not until much later, and by then I had fallen asleep on the couch. My mind was cranked up to a high, humming eleven out of ten, and my dreams were nauseous blurs. Deep closets and darkened movie theaters. White smiles and wriggling maggots. Around and around, carousel shadows. It was her stillness I felt, her utter, looming stillness that woke me.

I opened my eyes and she was standing over the couch. The muted television was the only light inside the house, and the living room came and went each time the screen flickered. My mother stared down at me from somewhere far, far back in her head. There was no recognition in that stare, not even the false recognition that made me into my dead father. She looked down at me, and I could not be sure she saw anyone at all.

"Sylvia Plath stuck her head in the oven because she was sad. She wrote no more poetry after that." My mother's voice was as limp as the arms that hung at her sides. "Her son liked fish. He lived in Alaska. He liked fish, and he lived in Alaska, and he hung himself because he was sad."

Urine trickled down my mother's skinny legs and pattered on the carpet between her feet.

"Who are you?" she said. "What are you doing in my house?"

My earlier frustrations with her had fled. I got up from the couch and, putting an arm around her, gu ided her to the stairs. She continued to dribble as we walked.

"Who are you? Where are you taking me? Who are you?" Her fingers wrapped themselves around the railing and refused to let go. I unpeeled them, then pushed her on gently. Her bones felt like sticks underneath her skin. The stench of her piss was strong and wild. "Let me go or I'll scream," she said as I led her into her bedroom. No point taking her to the toilet now that she had already finished her business. Her diapers lay in a heap in the doorway. She must have taken them off intending to go to the bathroom— sometimes she still managed to do that on her own—or perhaps they'd simply been uncomfortable. I pulled her nightgown off over her head, then I used its fabric to dry her legs. I tossed the soiled clothes in the laundry and sat her down on the bed.

"Stay here."

I came back with baby wipes to find her crawling on the floor. She scooted away from me when I bent to pick her up, but I caught her by the hips. They were knobs, and they made a good handhold as I hoisted her onto the bed. It was easy to do because she was so light. She was like an empty suitcase, if suitcases came with kicking legs. I flipped her onto her back, brought her ankles together, and pinned them down with one hand while I opened the box of baby wipes. The kicking didn't stop but moved up her body. She wriggled whitely against the maroon sheets, and my mind turned helplessly to the dog from the park, the dog whose mouth had let out a gush of larvae. I cleaned the tops of her feet and between her toes. A high, delirious giggle leapt from her throat, and her arms stretched out wide over the mattress, like the arms of a cross. She bucked violently, her hips thrusting at the air, as I wiped up her legs.

All at once she went still.

"Virginia Woolf put pockets in her rocks and walked into the river. The river was cold, and she was not looking for fish. She was sad. I miss how you used to touch me."

I almost didn't hear her. I'd used up the first wipe and was reaching for the second, and when I finally processed what she'd said, I froze. Her right hand walked down the bedspread and stopped between her legs. She was looking at me. Her gaze was hard and bright and hungry.

"I get so lonely sometimes," she said, and with two fingers, parted the gray tuft of her pubic hair. "I think about you, and I get all wet."

"Jesus," I said. "Stop that."

But still I could not move. It was as if some engine had stalled inside me. She began to itch at herself, to dig, and as her fingertip slipped out of her vagina, a spider followed it on scuttling black legs. She did not appear to notice. If she did, she did not care. She moaned as the spider escaped her, and went on moaning as it climbed across her knuckles to the white of her inner thigh. Where I smashed it. I didn't think about doing so. I simply did. Some things are not allowable no matter the circumstance, and a fanged insect crawling on my mom was one of them. The spider twitched and struggled under my palm. I pushed down harder until the twitching stop. Using the baby wipe, I picked its broken body off of her leg. There was an angry red mark on her skin.

"You hurt me," she said. Her eyes were teary, confused.

"I'm sorry," I said, and I was. So terribly sorry. I backed out through the door, unable to look at her, and on my way down the hall, I stumbled into the bathroom to be sick. I did not come out again for a long time.

14

There's a gauzy, feverish fear that only visits in the middle of the night. It cannot survive in the day. It is too insubstantial to exist under the sun. This fear is dry and clinging; it brushes the back of your neck and tickles along your earlobe. It cannot be shaken off or slapped away. It is a cobweb, and when you are tangled up in it, everything else is too. The world is a fly ensnared by its threads.

I went back to my room. I shut the door behind me, walked to the bed, and sat down on the very edge. My phone was on the nightstand. The screen was cracked, had been for a while, but now that seemed significant, somehow. It wasn't just that the spiral pattern resembled a web, or that the web made me think of what was crumpled up in the baby wipe that I had thrown into the bathroom's trashcan. It was the word itself. Cracked. I needed to—

Mind the cracks, I thought, and I saw the crack between my mother's legs, the crack I had slipped out of into this world. I saw the spider that walked out of her, and how badly I wanted to believe the spider had come from my head, but the web of my fear was crawling now, squirming like my mother on her sheets, like maggots on cement, and all maggots eventually grew up to look like their mommies, to fly like the fly that had walked out of Mom's nose, there on the corner where I had kicked her cup of change.

"Everything's got a price," I said, looking down at my poisoned finger. "Everything's got a price."

I picked up my phone, and when I opened my last text message, Tiffany's number appeared at the center of the web. I was thinking in bugs, seeing in bugs, and everything around me conformed to my insect logic, my crawly, clingy fear.

I dialed her number—no matter that it was two in the morning and the sane world was fast asleep. I was awake and she would be too, thinking of me, her fly, while she licked the little lump behind her perfect smile.

There was a click as the line connected.

"What did you do to me?" I said.

A man's voice answered, "Thank you for calling Sunset Hills. We are sorry that no one is available to take your call right now, but if you leave your name and number, we promise to get in touch with you within one business day. Here at Sunset Hills, we understand how difficult it is to lose a loved one, and the challenges that come with managing such a loss."

I let my phone hand fall to my lap. Tiffany had given me the number for a funeral home. She had walked into my office, and before sitting in my chair, before opening her mouth, she had written down the number for a funeral home.

15

She had known I would call. That was the only explanation. She had known I would call, and she had wanted to send a message to me when I did.

I went to the bathroom, shut the toilet, and sat down on the lid. My hand was trembling as I took the crumpled baby wipe out of the trashcan and unfolded it, and my mind wandered to the balled-up poem I had thrown into the office closet, the poem I had never found . . .

The spider was a black lump the size of my thumbnail. It looked as though it were asleep rather than dead, hugging itself with all of its limbs. I reached down to poke it, then changed my mind. Use your tools, the doctor had said. I took a plastic flosser from the jar by the sink, and with its pointy toothpick handle, I unpeeled the spider's legs from the leaking bulb of its body. I didn't know what I was looking for, if I was looking for anything specific at all. I think, mostly, I just wanted to touch it. To show myself it was still there, that it hadn't evaporated from the world as soon as I let it out of my sight. I kept on with my delicate surgery until the spider was spread out on full display.

Some of its legs had broken off partway, but none of them had been pulled out by the root. There were twelve legs in total, *twelve*, and every kid on Earth knows that spiders only come with eight.

I folded up the baby wipe.

I was beginning to worry that I was not losing my mind, after all.

PART TWO
THE OTHER
SIDE

16

The next morning I walked out the moment I heard tires in the driveway. My mother was in her office typing away under the quilt I had thrown around her shoulders. She hadn't dressed after wetting herself, and I hadn't been able to bring myself to dress her, so I stopped to warn Cassie that there might be one very old and very naked woman in her near future.

"That gal can let her tits hang out all she wants," she said. "As long as she doesn't get cold it's no bother to me. I've got all the same equipment."

With that came an image of Cassie lying in my mother's bed, dark against the dark sheets, while I wiped her legs clean. I scrubbed the thought away as I had done to the urine in the living room carpet, but some discomfort must have showed on my face because Cassie's eyebrows drew in closer to one another.

"Last night was a bad one, wasn't it?"

"No, no, it was fine." My right hand was buried in my pocket. I pulled it out along with the dried baby wipe. I'd planned this to look like an afterthought on my part, no big deal, but as soon as I started to unfold the wipe, I realized exactly how ridiculous the whole thing appeared. "Oh, I found this in my mom's bedroom. I was wondering if it might be poisonous."

Cassie stared down at the arachnid—if it could be classified as that with twelve legs—and said, "What might be poisonous?"

I'd expected Cassie not to see the spider just as the people in the park hadn't seen the maggots, but hearing her answer still dropped a large stone down my throat. I feigned surprise, quickly returning the wipe to my pocket. "Shit, damn thing must have fallen out. Whatever. It's dead anyway."

Cassie was looking at me strangely, and who could blame her? The wind, slight that morning but chilly, played with the purple tail of her scarf. Her lips were the soft dark red of a Merlot, and despite everything, I wanted to taste them. "What happened last night, Mike?"

"Nothing. Nothing happened." I smiled and as a joke I added, "Including sleep."

She didn't seem to find it funny.

"Tonight will be better," she said, adjusting the strap on her left shoulder. The strap belonged to a backpack. Why had she packed a backpack? Then I remembered. Today was Wednesday, and on Wednesday . . .

"Chinese food," I said.

"That's right." Her smile came out, just a little. She backed toward the house in her heeled shoes. "See you when you get home."

I walked to the train station, thinking not of what was in my pocket or of what lay ahead, but of how wonderful that word sounded coming out of Cassie's mouth.

Home.

Home.

Home.

17

Mom was home, too, sitting on her corner underneath the browned marquis. She did not look surprised to see me, only sad, though I wasn't sure if she ever looked any other way. I held out the crumbled baby wipe. "Open it. Please. Tell me what you see."

She opened it. Closed it. Handed it back to me. "You've caught yourself a spider. One of His." She said *His* with a capital H, as if she were talking about God, but I was too overwhelmed by the enormity of her seeing the spider to process anything else. I wasn't crazy. What I was I did not know, but I was not crazy.

"It came out of my mother's—it came crawling out of my mother. And yesterday in the park I watched a dog puke up maggots like he couldn't even feel them, like he was a faucet and somebody turned him on. And you—"

Before I could finish, Mom reached up calmly and stuck the tips of two yellow-nailed fingers into one ear. She dug around and then pulled them out. Pinched between them was a struggling housefly. "The old and the sick are the first to crack. The closer we get to death, the thinner we become, and I am not speaking about our flesh and bones."

"What the hell *are* you speaking about?"

Mom waited for a loud truck to rumble by on Beacon. "Do you ever itch, Mike? Do you ever feel a scamper down your backside, but when you scratch it, nothing's there? You're wrong, you know. There *is* something there. The whole world is crawling with His children."

"Whose children?"

She squashed the fly between her fingers. "Nobody sees them. They are like all of us, out here, are to all of you."

"*Whose* children?"

The old woman looked up at the gray March sky, and though her face was already dimmed by the marquis, I could have sworn I saw a shadow fall over it, a deep rolling shadow, as of a cloud passing overhead.

"I'm so sorry," she said. "I have done a terrible thing, and if I could take it back, I would."

I was getting no answers, so this time I did not give her a question. "You sent her. That girl. You sent her after me."

"No," she said after a moment. "I went to her after what you did. I went to her with my pain, but I did not send her. I did not have to."

The connection was obvious, which was why I hadn't seen it earlier. We all called her Mom because she called everyone her child, but I'd never considered she might have a child of her own.

"She's your daughter. Tiffany. If that's really her name."

She blinked in surprise and said, almost defensively, "It's not."

"What did she do to me? What did that thing in her mouth do to me?" My bad finger throbbed so hard that the skin of my hand itched.

Again, my questions received no answer.

I got down on one knee. "Listen, please. You have to tell me what's happening. If you're sorry at all, like you say you are, you have to tell me what's happening to me."

She did not speak for a while. When she did, her voice was soft. "Everything you know, everything you love, is laminate. The ground you walk on, the air you breathe, the place you call your home, it is all laminate, and soon you will see what is on the other side, if you have not glimpsed it already. Very soon."

I got up. I was shaking. With fear, yes, but with anger too. "What I did to you, you've already paid me back for. Call it off now. Make it stop."

"There is no calling it off. It's done."

"Like fuck it's done. This is my *life*. This is my fucking *life*."

Beacon was getting busy. Cars on the sidewalks, people on the streets. The rush hour noise of a world that was beginning to feel further and further from my own.

Mom looked up at me sadly from her shadow under the marquis.

And said nothing.

18

I went to work. While Lucy gave my first appointment the old floss and fluoride one-two, I slipped behind her desk and pulled out the portfolio where she kept patient information before adding it to the database in our computer. Tiffany had been in last, so her page was sitting right on top. I don't know what I was hoping to find—some clue about her, I suppose—but she'd only given her first name, which I'd just discovered to be an alias, and the phone number for Sunset Hills Funeral Home. Next to the number she had drawn a smiley face. Seeing that, I discovered something about myself.

There was room in my heart, a whole room that had gone unfurnished until now, for hate.

"Mike?" said Lu. "Shawna is ready."

Shawna was a nine year old girl who had been coming to my office ever since her mother and father moved to Boston from Chicago two years ago. She had long black braided hair capped by bright blue beads that made noise whenever she moved. This morning she also had a cavity, and as I was filling it in, the beads in her hair tinkled ever so slightly with her extreme effort to keep still. My drill blocked out all outside sound, but I could still hear the silent throb of my finger—a thudthudthud that made the bones in my hand feel like flimsy drumsticks . . . and was the redness beginning to creep down past the bottom knuckle? I thought so, though it was hard to tell through my latex glove.

"Owwowww," Shawna said.

"Shoot—sorry." My drill had slipped and nicked her gums. Just a tiny gash, barely a bleeder, but I had lost my grip on the slippery trust that is essential to convincing people—even kids—to let you wield a power tool inside their mouth. I took out her jaw prop. "I done goofed, and when I done goof, I believe firmly in making up for it." *Everything's got a price,* I almost said. I rolled my chair back with a push and took a sucker from the top drawer of my desk. "Sugar got you into this mess, so I might be a bad dentist for saying this, but I happen to think sugar makes for a pretty mean pain reliever. What do you think?"

She nodded, the sucker lodged in her mouth. Her eyes, filmy with tears a moment ago, began to clear.

"All right, Shawna. Catch me up while you polish that off. How's school?"

Shawna talked about her teacher, Miss Bartholomew, and the library. Every kid was allowed to check out books, which were organized by reading level. She was in the third grade but could read red-stickered books that were meant for fifth graders, she told me proudly. There was a computerized program called A.R. that tested you on the story, and if you scored high enough you got points you could later exchange for toys and things. It was nice listening to her talk. My mom would have been glad to know at least some kids were still reading these days.

After the sucker was worn down to the stick, I finished dealing with the cavity. Shawna handled it bravely. I leaned over to remove her jaw prop for the final time and then paused. Something moved far back in her throat, below her tonsils. It walked in a low slither, and walk is what it did—on crawling hair-thin legs, it walked up her tongue and out of her mouth. Two scarlet antennas twitched on its hard black head, touching and feeling the path forward. Its body continued to come, spilling over her chin and down the bib on her shirt. Segment after segment, leg after leg after leg, it came, dark orange and shiny bright under the fluorescents.

Shawna sat up as I rolled my chair back. She looked at me in confusion, her mouth locked open, and still it had not stopped, still the thing was growing longer. With a flick, its pronged tail dragged itself out over her bottom lip, and three scuttling feet of centipede walked down her body onto the floor.

19

I told Shawna she was all set. I used those exact words— "All set!"—and ran out of the room. She came out a moment later, still wearing her jaw prop, and I intercepted her in the hall before her father could see her walking around looking like her face had been frozen open in the middle of the world's biggest yawn. He was a stay-at-home dad, and a good one from what I'd gathered. I strolled his way while Lu prepared Shawna's goodie bag (toothpaste, floss, and a report card that featured a smiling molar), and he stuck out a paw that could have fit on a bear. When I went to take it, I realized I was still wearing my latex gloves. Whoops. Silly me. By the time I peeled them off and shoved them in my pocket, the time frame for a handshake had expired. Which was fine by me. My finger didn't need any extra squeezing, especially not from someone who weighed three hundred pounds. At least.

"So, no more soda," he said with a sheepishness at odds with his sheer size. He thought I was going to scold him over his daughter's cavity. Serious business, cavities. Once they start, they just keep coming and coming and coming . . .

"Mike? You okay?"

Sure, I'm great. There's a mile-long centipede slither-walking around my office, and by the way, your nine-year old daughter has one hell of a good gag reflex.

"Tony," I said, and then wondered if that was even his name. I decided to roll with it. "Everything's probably fine. But I just want to make sure."

"Sure of what?" he said. His shoulders straightened, and he looked his weight class now, he sure did.

"Well, like I said, it's probably nothing. But I've been seeing Shawna for a couple years." Uncharted waters, no lifeboat in sight. "And her breath, well, there's something off in it."

"What do you mean *off?*"

It's crawling, I thought. "It's a little . . . sweet. I don't know how to explain better. I've got a good nose but a lackluster vocabulary. My mom used to have me sniff her wines at dinner." Why was I telling him that? He didn't want to know that. "Just do me a favor, will you? Get her checked out. Today, if you can."

"Because her breath is sweet."

I prayed that Shawna wouldn't mention I'd been wearing a mask over my mouth and nose during our appointment. "I don't even know if 'sweet' is the right word. I just smelled something off, and—"

The old and the sick are the first to crack.

"Shawna's fine," he said in a voice that had dropped a few registers. "She's a healthy young girl."

"I'm sure you're right." I heard beads tinkling our way. My window was almost up. "But it doesn't hurt to be safe, does it?"

Tony stared down at me, his jaws working under his beard. Then he smiled a broad smile, scooped up his daughter, and said, "How's your tooth, hon?"

"Hurts."

"I'm sorry. That's no fun." He carried her out the door into the fresh morning drizzle. He did not glance back.

20

I went to hunt down Shawna's hitchhiker with a broom and a lidded dust pan, but the centipede was nowhere to be found. It hadn't crawled under the desk, and it wasn't hiding under the cabinets (these I looked under on hands and knees from a safe distance, shining the flashlight on my phone). That left the supply closet in the back of the room. The door was cracked open. I took the knob . . .

. . . and pushed the door shut.

I had no concrete reason for ending my search there, but I did anyway. Part of it was the uneasy memory of the office closet back home. The other part was harder to define. As I'd stood there holding the knob, I'd gotten the sense that beyond the door wasn't an inside but an *out*side. Rain drummed the roof of the building, making a gentle background noise that echoed all around . . . except in the closet. In the closet, I heard emptiness. Sighing emptiness, like wind over a valley.

So I shut the door.

Then I dragged the throw rug out from behind my desk and pressed its edge flush to the crack underneath. Just in case.

21

By lunch I felt like a screw hole that had seen too many screws. I was worn down inside, stripped clean. Not because anything else happened after Shawna, but because I was waiting for something to happen. Every mouth, before it opened, held back a squirming flood. Every throat was a tunnel down which blind, chitinous things slithered toward the light.

I left my food in my bag and went out for a smoke, walking through the bare concrete hallway that my office shares with the neighboring businesses in the building. Out back I stood under the balcony and watched the rain pound itself into a fine mist against the ground. Puddles formed on the asphalt. Fattened cardboard bulged from the dumpster. March was showing its other cheek this afternoon, and nothing under its great bluish gray bruise would stay dry. Except, maybe, for Mom on her corner. The storm would know better than to fuck with her.

"What did you do to me?" I said, breathing smoke out of my nose. But that wasn't the right question. The right question was, what was *I* going to do? I killed my first cigarette under my heel and then lit a second. As a rule, I held myself to one a day. Today I intended to have them all.

That's what I did. I smoked my pack empty in silence, feeling as alone as a man can feel in a city full of people, and when I was down to the last butt, I walked over to the dumpster to throw away my trash. The rain had paused, and the stillness it left behind was naked, newly born. I started the way I had come, going slowly over the wet asphalt. Was I going to go right back to work, drilling, capping, cleaning teeth, hopping around on my one foot as if everything were normal? Was that what I was going to do?

I paused, not sure why at first. My head turned to the pool of water by my foot.

The puddle swam with red. I saw myself silhouetted on its surface. Above my reflection stretched a hazy crimson sky shot through by brilliant white stars. Lifting my head, I looked up into the blue-gray cloudbank over Boston. Then I looked back down into that other sky mirrored below me. That *night* sky. Dizzy, I shut my eyes and stumbled away, but still I could see those stars burning hot in their bloodied firmament, shining down on . . .

Where?

Where?

Good God, *where?*

My echoing footsteps chased me down the corridor to my office. Lucy was waiting anxiously for me, and no wonder. The clock above my desk read a quarter of one, which meant I was fifteen minutes late for my first afternoon appointment.

"Hey," she said. "Where have you—"

My expression silenced her, and I inserted my voice into the pause. "I have to go. Something's come up. With my— my mom."

"Oh *no*. Mike. I'm so sorry."

"I won't be back for the rest of the week." I wouldn't be back next week, either. My career as a dentist, my life as a working adult, had come to an end. I just did not know it yet.

"Of course," she said. "I'll take care of everything here. You don't have to worry."

I barely heard what she said. I walked through the waiting room without a glance at the boy and woman sitting there, and a moment later I was headed down Beacon toward Mom on her corner. She sat far back under the marquis, and sure enough, the rain had not touched her. Flies walked the dry, wrinkled skin of her face . . . and if I looked closely at them, if I picked apart their bodies under a microscope, what would I find? A spare, vestigial wing buried in their soft black flesh? A dozen glossy eyes peeking out from their bellies?

"My sweet child," she said. "You saw it, didn't you?"

"I don't know what I saw, and I don't care. I just want it to end. The whole thing. All of it. Take it back."

"There is no taking it back."

"You keep saying that. You keep saying it's done, like I should just drop it and go away, thank you very much. But I'm still here, and I'm not going away." My temples were pounding. A vein had asserted itself along my hairline. I could feel my heart beating inside it, and everywhere else in my body where blood moved. "You're going to help me, and if you won't, or can't, then your daughter will."

She did not flinch. But she did not speak for a moment either. "You'll never find her. And even if you did—"

"It wouldn't make a difference, I know. See, I'm listening. But you aren't, and you need to start right now. I'll find her, I will, and you'd both better hope she's got something more to say than 'sorry.' Because you overpaid. You hear me? You and your bitch daughter overpaid, and you'll make it right or I am going to owe you some goddamn *change*."

I dropped the crumpled baby wipe, with the dead spider wrapped inside, into her money cup.

She looked down into the cup for a few long seconds. As she lifted her face, her lips spread into a horrible, joyless grin. For every one of her yellowing teeth, there was a tiny bulge in her gums. The deep red flesh of her mouth was fat with secret lumps. "They're small right now, the cracks, but they will widen . . . oh, they will widen."

22

I didn't have a plan, but I had five hours and I was desperate. At least I thought I was. In truth, desperation and I were little more than passing acquaintances. We hadn't yet become the close friends we are now.

Tiffany—which was still how I thought of her—was a young woman who had no doubt grown up hard. Nevertheless, she took reasonably good care of herself. She combed her hair and brushed her teeth, and she was no stranger to floss either. Judging by the way she spoke, she'd also seen the inside of a book or two. That might have been a reach (growing up with my mom had taught me to automatically classify everyone I met as a reader or non-reader), but I didn't think so. She was intelligent. Schooled, even. And cold. Couldn't forget that. She also had access to cash, and not the kind that comes from rattling a cup on a corner. Between her money and her tired clothing, I had previously guessed she worked the streets as well as lived on them. But if Boston had a clandestine red light district, I didn't have the first idea how to find it let alone how to find *her* once I did. Boston didn't even allow strip clubs within city limits, or sorority housing because of some ancient puritanical by law instituted to safeguard against brothels, so any illicitness would have to be buried deep underground, and I had no means to go about digging. Which left me with nothing but my memory of her appearance, and even that was flimsy. She'd been tall, she'd been slender, and she'd worn a ponytail that had tightened the skin over her prominent cheekbones, but her hair might have been anything from sandy blond to black . . . and her eyes, I remembered the chill of them but not their color. Tiffany was a nice face and a set of straight, white teeth that grew larger and brighter the more I thought of her until they became all I could see.

Traveling east on Beacon away from Mom and her corner, my fear and anger seething like venom through my bloodstream, I walked myself into a state that was close to panic. I did not consider taking the train. I did not think at all except that I had to find her, find Tiffany, find the girl, the girl, the girl. Gutters overflowed. Lazy rivers ran along curbsides. Rooftops dripped quietly. On the sidewalks and in the streets were puddles, laid out like mirrors that shattered with every passing footstep, every car, splashing their broken reflections up into the air. I kept my gaze on a strict upward slant and gave a wide berth to every pool of water. There was only one sky I wanted to look at, and it was the sky I had grown up beneath, the gray-blue, unhappy sky over Boston, my city, my *home*.

Three or so miles sit between my office and downtown, and I went the whole distance in a fast, blind stroll one gear below a jog. The exertion worked enough panic out of my system that I began to see my surroundings again. I passed Berklee, the music school my grandparents wanted me to go to the instant I picked up a sax in the fourth grade (the sax stayed behind when I graduated elementary, but my grandparents never completely relinquished their dreams of me becoming the next Charlie Parker), and there in the trendy, shop-centric corner of town my mother called Yuppieville, I started my search in earnest. Only fat wallets and tourists came to this part of Boston, so the homeless did too, like parched impala to a watering hole. I wandered the streets until the streets blurred and the faces on them ran together—eyes, noses, talking mouths and teeth, teeth, teeth. I went to the public library at Copley, thinking that if Tiffany had an education, maybe she'd come by it here where it was free, but I did not see her behind any computer or down any aisle. Truth be told, if I *had* stumbled upon her, I doubt I would have recognized her. I'd have had a hard time picking myself out of a lineup the way I was that afternoon.

I left the library but went no further east. That direction was the Common, and Tiffany would just have to be somewhere else because I would not be going there again. The green line took me to the red, and the red took me to Cambridge, where I explored the old brick alleyways of Harvard Square. I saw men and women huddled in soaked cardboard houses. I saw beatnik teenagers playing drums on upside-down buckets. I saw a scrawny man by a tall wire caddy full of trash bags argue with himself passionately while flies made a thick, swarming beard on his face. I saw a mother rock her sleeping baby, and through the crack of the baby's mouth, I saw legs—long, black, prickly legs— struggling to escape.

I saw far more than I wanted to.

I rode the train home with my head in my hands and my heart between my feet.

23

"You smell like you fucked an ashtray," Cassie said when I walked through the door. I told her I was sorry but really I was glad. You know how it feels to step into a warm house after spending too much time out in the cold? Seeing her was like that. She had on light blue leggings and a white cotton t-shirt that seemed to touch her breasts and no other part of her. She also had on the severest, most disapproving scowl I've ever seen, but in the same way that an insincere smile won't reach a person's eyes, this scowl fell short of hers. "There's only one solution, Mike," she said, and reached into her backpack. Her hand came out holding a bottle of baby soap. "You're going to have to take that bubble bath. And before you start up with your protests, I want to make one thing perfectly clear. I'm not asking."

I'd like to make a few things clear as well. I hadn't eaten since the piece of buttered toast I'd shoved down for breakfast, and only through sheer, stubborn, masculine refusal to show weakness was I able to stand on my feet without moaning. I should also mention that each time Cassie opened her mouth, I flinched inwardly, expecting something to crawl out of it. If something had, there wouldn't have been enough left of me to tell this story. My mind would have given like dry kindling under a boot heel, and that would have been the end of it all right at that moment. But nothing came out of her, nor did anything unordinary happen for the rest of the night.

"Fine," I said. "You win."

"I know. Now get a move on while I order us some Kung Pao."

"What if I don't like Kung Pao? What if I want orange chicken?"

"You'll eat what I tell you to eat," she said. "And be sure to tiptoe, will you? Your mom just settled down for her nap."

There was a C.D. player in the bathroom—no, I'm not joking. The thing must have predated the new millennium. When I turned it on, some really soul-stirring stuff came through the speakers stationed on the sink and toilet. "Enya," I said, switching it off with a shudder. "You've got to be kidding me."

By the music station was an uncorked bottle of wine and a single glass that I filled well past the point of etiquette. The hopeful part of me—or maybe the presumptuous part—was a bit deflated that Cassie hadn't laid out *two* glasses. Oh well. I peeled off my clothes as the tub filled and the mirror grew foggy. Nothing showed in the reflection but me, and that was a scary enough sight. Fifteen pounds had fallen off my already lean frame since I'd moved back home, and my bones were playing peekaboo through my skin, which was so sun deprived it was en-route to becoming translucent. My hair needed a date with scissors like I needed a full night's sleep, and my beard brought to mind the man I had seen in Harvard Square, the man whose face had been covered in flies.

I settled down into the sudsy, rising water with my wine. The heat was nothing short of glorious, and the bubbles tickled me deliciously in places I hadn't been tickled for far too long. I sipped the Cabernet, dreaming of the dark fruit of

Cassie's lips, wondering if she would sleep in the guest bed tonight or if, perhaps . . .

The door opened.

Cassie closed and locked it behind her. "The food is on the way. I figure we have twenty minutes as long as a certain somebody stays asleep." She pulled off her shirt, slid out of her leggings, and walked to me smoothly across the tiled floor.

So.

That answered that.

24

Her nipples were soapy and bittersweet, and her skin was slick as oil against mine. By the time we finished, there was more water outside the tub than there was in it. We lay together in the little bit that was left, our bodies overheated, our breaths coming hard and fast.

"You have no clue," she said, "how long I've wanted that."

"I think I have an idea."

We dried ourselves and the bathroom the best we could, which was not very well at all seeing as the delivery guy began to knock on the door downstairs. The noise woke my mother, who went down to let him in, forgetting once more that locked doors did not open unless you had a key. Soon the three of us were seated around the kitchen table, faced by a dozen steaming boxes of Chinese.

"Goodness, you are pretty," my mother told Cassie. "What is your name?"

"Cassandra."

"What a lovely name! My name is Bev, and most people think that's short for Beverly, but it isn't. I'm just Bev, but you can take away the 'just' when you think of me because 'just' is the nastiest word in the English language. It makes less of whatever's near it, and nothing's going to do that to me. Goodness, you are pretty. I'd kiss you on the lips if you asked."

"Well, I'd better not ask then because I don't know if I could control myself after a kiss from you."

This was a conversation they'd had before many times, and Cassie's remark enamored my mom into temporary speechlessness as it always did. "And who is this?" she said to me. Tonight I was a friendly stranger, and that was a comfortable someone to be. "Are you her fellow?"

Cassie had served herself a dollop of white rice and was busy poking through the other containers. Her search paused.

"I don't know," I said. "I hope so."

Cassie gave no outward sign she'd heard me, but she went back to looking through the toppings with, I thought, the slightest more ease to her movements. She grunted as she opened the last container. "Fuck."

"What?"

"I forgot to order Kung Pao."

25

Later, after my mother had fallen asleep and Cassie and I had made love a second, slower, sweeter time, we lay in bed wearing nothing but the keys to the house around our necks. The lamp on the nightstand touched us and us alone. All else was dark.

"You men are lucky," said Cassie.

"How's that?"

"You will never know the pain of having soap in the vagina."

"Baby soap."

"Still."

"What about soap in the dick?" I asked, stroking the low of her back. Our legs were laced so that it was difficult to tell where one of us ended and the other began.

"Small point of entry, and an excellent purge function."

"Fair."

She said nothing for a little while. "You looked tired when you came home tonight, Mike. You always look tired, but today it was like you just got back from a week in the Bush."

"How do I look now?"

"Much better," she said, planting a kiss on my ear. But she wasn't about to let me escape that easily. "What's going on with you?"

"It's just been a hard week at work, mostly." The key word of that sentence, mostly, inserted itself after a pause. Cassie sat up on an elbow to look down at me.

"Mike."

"Well, the infection for one." I held up my right hand. The forefinger was showing no signs of improvement despite a day and a half of heavy antibiotics. Not that I had expected it to, but I couldn't hide the ugly thing so I figured I might as well lay as much blame on it as possible.

"And for two?" she said.

I didn't respond.

Cassie licked the front of her teeth, something she did only when she was in serious thought. "Mike, did I ever tell you why I got into the field of degenerative brain disease?"

"Your grandpa, was it?"

"Yes and no. I was sixteen when he got Alzheimer's. God, I hate that word. Got. It makes it sound like he woke up with the illness one day, like it was a cold or something. He moved in with me and my dad, and I got—there it is again—I got to watch him get worse. Hell, even in the past tense that word is chasing me." Cassie gave a small, distracted laugh. "Most people think they *get* everything about me right there, that I studied DBD because of what it did to my grandpa, and I let them go on thinking that because it's easier, and maybe because it sounds nicer than the truth. My grandpa, he broke my dad, and I hated him for it. He wore him down day by day until my dad looked like the old empty skin a snake crawls out of and leaves behind, and then Grandpa got sick-sick on top of it, and the medical bills took what was left. I'm not saying my dad *died*—nothing dramatic like that—but he never got back a sniff of what he gave up. Which was fine. He knew what he was signing up for from the beginning.

Look, I know this probably sounds like I've got some sort of complex, like I got into caretaking to 'save' people because I couldn't save my dad, but it's not. I don't blame my grandpa, and I don't regret wanting to shove him down the stairs sometimes. I was a kid. All I'm saying is I know how hard it is and you don't have to take it all on alone."

I nodded, and I meant for that to be the end of the conversation, I really did. But there were cracks in me, as, I suppose, there are cracks in all of us, and that evening mine were opened wide. I said, "Last night. Mom wet herself."

Cassie was quiet.

"She woke me up in the living room—I'd fallen asleep down there—and when I took her upstairs to change her, clean her, she started saying things. Touching herself. She thought I was someone else. My dad, or someone after my dad. I know that. I *know* that, but—"

I ran out of voice. Cassie finished for me. "But it was not what one would call a good time."

"No," I said, and laughed suddenly, hoarsely. "No, it was not."

Cassie ran her finger along my collarbone, lightly tracing the dip over my throat. "Have you ever heard of the fundamental attribution error? Don't answer. I'm going to tell you about it anyway. In shorthand, it's called situational bias, which amounts to our tendency to credit a person's behavior to who they are *inside* rather than outside stimulus. Like where they are or who they're with. If a girl acts chilly at a party, she's a bitch. We don't stop to wonder if she's got social anxiety or if she's put off that her ex-boyfriend is tonguing his new girlfriend in the next room. I know, Cassie, what's the point? Well, every person you meet is potentially a lot of different people depending on the circumstance, the environment, and about a hundred other variables. So if you keep that consideration in mind and extend it to somebody like your mom who often forgets the whens, whats, wheres, and whos in her life, then you're looking at the possibility of all sorts of personalities at any given moment. I met one eighty-five year old lady who spent most of her time thinking she was seventeen and it was prom night. Every guy who stepped into her room became her date. They'd have to give her a long, appreciating look and follow it up with a peck on the cheek or she'd be so affronted she wouldn't speak to them. Not a single word. It's funny, you know, there's all this hoopla in the media about DID—Dissociative Identity Disorder—when in fact it's really rare. The true king of multiple personalities is degenerative brain disease and it's sitting right under all our noses."

"Thank you," I said after a moment.

"What for?" she asked distantly, still caught in the professor side of her brain, dreaming up connections and hypotheses in front of a busy chalkboard.

"Most people ask if I have a sister or an aunt somewhere, or tell me it's such a shame I don't. Like it's not normal, me looking after my mother. Like it's not my place, not a *man's* place, and I should feel bad for doing the stuff I have to do. For seeing her the way I see her. But you never did."

Cassie pushed herself up so that her key dangled over mine. She took my hand and laid the palm over her breast.

You can guess what I felt beating underneath it. "Your place is with the people you care about," she said, "and the people who care about you. Nowhere else."

We made love again, and this time neither of us came. But that was all right, because without a finish line to cross, we never stopped, not really. We simply moved from moving into sleep, with me inside her and her holding onto me.

26

I slept through the night and in the morning I felt rested if not ready for the day. Cassie kissed me goodbye, and I left the way I always left for work, taking the red to the green and the green to Allston, where I got off one stop earlier than normal so that I could approach the crossing of Beacon and Harvard Avenue from a distance without being seen.

Yesterday, I had let my fear run me on a wild hunt all around town. But I was never going to be able to search every alley or underpass, or knock on every door in every shelter. If I was going to find Tiffany, I would have to start with the one and only actual connection I had to her, which was the old woman sitting on her corner underneath her weathered marquis. Tiffany loved her mother. Enough to kill for her. Enough, maybe, to do even worse. That meant they were close. I needed to learn everything I could about Mom.

I needed to watch.

There's a coffee shop on Beacon called Slow Drip, and it pours the good stuff unlike the nearby Dunkin Donuts on Harvard Ave. I ordered some dark roast and settled down at the counter by the window looking out on Mom's corner. She was half a block away plus an intersection—just close enough for me to make out the flies going walkabout on her face. From a distance they looked like roving flecks of shadow. Mom herself was a blanketed lump with a bit of toothy whiteness where her skin showed. The sun had made a rare appearance this morning, but its light left her alone as the rain had left her alone yesterday. I watched her for an unbroken—almost unblinking—fifteen minutes, and she did not once stir. My coffee tasted like untempered fossil fuel. Perfect, in other words. I settled in for the long haul.

Places like Slow Drip expect people to rent a seat for hours, but they might have thought it odd if I spent the whole day staring out of the window like a house cat, so back home I'd grabbed a book off the shelf and stuffed it into my bag. When I saw what chance had selected for me, my stomach did a slow, uneasy somersault.

My Hungry Friend
A Memoir by Bev Jacoby.

The cover showed a skyline whose buildings and clouds all bore a suggestion of teeth, as if something had been nibbling on them idly. I flipped past the copyright page and stopped on the dedication:

"To my son, Michael, whose hand is always there for me when I am lost."

For a moment I forgot where I was and what I was doing there, and as my surroundings came back to me, something else surfaced with them, like a tentacled creature dragged up from the dark of an underwater canyon. A question I hadn't allowed myself to consider until now: what would happen to my mother if I could not stop what was happening to me? Who would take care of her if I no longer could? Cassie? No. She had signed up for a job, not an anchor tied to her waist. That left the one thing I had been trying to avoid from the beginning, which was a facility, but those also required money. Not to mention the time needed to make the arrangements, and how much time did I have exactly before . . . ?

"Enough," I said shakily. "Enough."

Yesterday's storm had backed up the drain in front of Slow Drip. Dead maggots floated around the black mouth of the gutter. I turned my eyes back to Mom and kept them there. Every now and then I flipped a page in the book and took a sip of coffee. I finished my first cup at 7:30. Still Mom hadn't so much as turned her head. By noon I was onto my fourth cup, and I was starting to wonder if she was even breathing. I took a piss in the restroom and returned to my watchpost. Another hour crawled by and nothing happened except for the occasional person pausing to drop a few coins into Mom's cup. Caffeine had my skull in a vice. My teeth were grinding. My fingers tapped the back of my mother's book. My toes curled and uncurled inside my loafers.

Around two o'clock, the door to Dunks opened and Napkin Guy walked out carrying a paper rose. He gave the rose to Mom, who held it up to take a long sniff before handing it back to him. He seemed pleased, though I couldn't see more than his posture. The shoulders under his heavy coat gave a light bounce, a laughing bounce, and he bent over to pick up her change cup. He took the cup back with him into Dunks and a few minutes later emerged with a sandwich wrapped in greasy white paper. He passed the food to her along with her cup (now empty), which got knocked over by the breeze. Seven hours of watching, and I had learned that Mom did in fact eat. That wasn't much, but it was a start. I wondered if Napkin Guy knew about the lumps in her mouth, and what was hiding in them. My eyes strayed back down to the book in my hands and picked out a random line.

"My hungry friend has no friends but me, and no taste for anything that is not mine."

Mom nibbled through her meal, and it dawned on me that her appetite was only the first of *two* things that I had learned about her. She belonged to a community, one that was right there to see but so often overlooked. If Napkin Guy helped feed her, it stood to reason that their relationship might stretch further . . . say, to a first and last name basis. Perhaps I'd have to have another chat with him at some point.

The next couple hours passed quietly, underlined by the soft jazz playing inside the coffeehouse. Somebody brought in a laptop and set about attacking the keys, turning my mind to my mother's typewriter and the crumpled poem I had thrown into the closet. Where had the poem gone? *There* was a question, and once it came to me, I saw that the question was but a reflection in a mirror. Turn it around, look at it the other way, and it became not about that crumpled ball of paper but about the maggots in the gutter, the flies on Mom's face. Instead of "where had the poem gone?" I was now staring at "where had those things come *from*?" The twelve-legged spider, the three-foot centipede . . . they did not belong to Earth. So where did they belong?

I shut my eyes and waiting for me in the dark was a red night sky full of blazing white stars.

The sun set behind gauzy clouds, and Boston dimmed under the filtered light. Five o'clock, the end of my work day, was fast approaching. Cassie would be expecting me home soon. I put *My Hungry Friend* back into my bag and stood up to leave when Mom's arm emerged from her blankets. At first it appeared she was resting her head on one hand, then I saw the blue sliver between her palm and ear. A phone. Mom had a phone.

I sat back down. All the coffee I'd had that day was nothing next to this discovery. My head hummed and whirled. Mom had a phone, and phones did not work unless someone was paying the bill. That was a law of nature, right up there with gravity. And who else would be paying the bill if not the same person who paid that other bill, to me, for the cruel and unthinking thing I had done . . . who, but her sweet, loyal daughter?

"You *do* have a phone, Tiffany. You're on it right now, aren't you?"

Mom stayed on the line for ten minutes. If I'd been a betting man, I would have put my savings down that she and Tiffany talked this way, at this time, every day. Just how I was going to follow this lead, I wasn't sure yet, but it was something. I got up to take one last trip to the restroom, feeling the way a bloodhound must feel when he catches the scent. Slow Drip has a short back hallway that sits at a perpendicular angle to the coffee shop itself, and normally this little nook is cheerfully bright, but today the overhead was out and the hallway was as dim as Mom's corner under Boston's slow, choked nightfall. I bumped the restroom door open with my shoulder. More often than not, that was enough to trigger the motion sensors and activate the lights. Not this time. I reached inside to wave my arm. Still, no light. The air inside the restroom felt warm, humid, compared to the air in the hallway. My first thought was that someone had just dropped some napalm in there (don't ask how I've come by this knowledge, but a ferocious bowel movement can make any confined space feel like Tennessee in the middle of the summer). A tentative sniff set off no alarm bells, however. I smelled only the coffee on my breath and what reminded me vaguely of my mother's garden. A lush, soily odor with an underlining of something vegetal. My ears tuned into a gentle, deep swishing, and my eyes picked up on the softest flickers of red in the restroom. The dark shifted, swayed, changing and changing but staying always the same. I leaned forward. The swishing was coming from somewhere up above, along with the flickers, which never touched the walls or floor. I could not see the walls or floor at all.

Shadows, I thought, *the dark is made of moving shadows*.

Some part of me continued to cling stubbornly to the idea of the motion sensors. I waved my arm again. Nothing. I reached for the light switch, and here I must be as precise as possible. I was standing in the doorway with one arm, my right arm, extended into the restroom. The switch rested to the left of the doorway, about chest height on the wall. I knew this. I had used the switch earlier. The switch was not there anymore. Neither was the wall. Where both had been, my hand touched empty space. Sweat popped on my forehead. My guts rolled up like baker's dough. The outside of the wall was there—I was staring at it—but the *inside* of the wall was not.

It had ceased to exist.

By this point my body had turned in the doorway so that I faced the frame head on, half of me in the restroom—in the dark—and half of me in the hall. I moved my hand another inch. My fingers passed the plane of the wall without any resistance. They should have been poking out of the woodwork into the corridor, but they weren't. They were still in that place where the air was humid and great, gentle shadows let through shafts of hazy red light. I reached further, my elbow bending as I did, and I was feeling some real resistance now, you'd better believe I was, but the resistance was purely in my head. The tethers that bound me to reality had begun to snap. I gripped the wall with my left hand to keep my feet flat on the ground, but the act of touching—feeling—with one part of me what I was reaching through with another part buckled the last uprights in my brain. I saw and felt the rest from worlds away, and maybe that wasn't such an exaggeration. No, maybe that wasn't such an exaggeration at all.

My arm continued to curl inward until nearly all of it had passed through the wall. I was hugging myself, except I wasn't. My fingers should have been touching my opposite shoulder, except they weren't. The space I occupied in the hall was not the same space that my fingers explored. At last they met something solid past where my shoulder was (wasn't), something that my reeling mind insisted was inside my ribcage, near my frantically beating heart.

Bark.

Damp, bloated bark.

The final connections slid into place. Bark belonged to trees, and so those great lazy shadows were the shadows of leaves, enormous leaves, forming a canopy under the sky. Outside. Inside the restroom was outside, and the light that fell there was red.

Warmth oozed over my knuckles, and only my clenched jaws saved me from screaming. I pulled my hand out through the doorway. Carefully. Sap, sticky and black and loathsome, dripped down my fingers. I didn't stop to wipe it off. I grabbed my things and ran out into the cool dusk of a world slipping toward night, and as I headed away down Beacon, away from Mom on her corner, one relentless thought pursued me ahead of all others:

If I'd simply darted from the restroom, if I hadn't first pulled my arm out through the doorway, would I still have my arm with me? Or would I have left it behind in that place where leaves as large as sailboats rocked underneath an alien sky?

27

I was good and late when I got back to Savin Hill, but I took another ten minutes to collect myself, sitting on one of the swings in the park by the boardwalk. Night had fallen over Quincy Bay, and the waves were something I heard but did not see. I felt as if I were sitting on the edge of Earth, looking out over a vast, dark unknown.

Cassie didn't stick around after I got home. I told her that there'd been a snag in my last appointment, which reminded me of the snaggletooth in Tiffany's mouth, which brought out the throb in my finger so badly I wanted to grit my own teeth. I kept waiting for her to ask what was wrong, but thankfully she never did. She'd been in the house for going on thirty-six hours and was becoming a mite stir crazy.

"You wouldn't believe how many times your old gal turned the stovetop on," she vented, and I said that I didn't envy her. My right hand was still gooey with black sap (I had wiped and wiped but nothing short of a hot, soapy scrub would do the job), and on a whim I laced my fingers through Cassie's. We said our goodbyes after a kiss and a promise to do last night again soon. I watched her go down the driveway to her car. As she did, she absently rubbed the hand I had been holding on her leggings.

As if she'd gotten something on it.

Something sticky.

I locked the front door with the key around my neck. For the next few hours I thought of Mom, her phone, and the man with the paper flowers who brought her food so she never had to leave her corner. I went to bed early, hoping to sleep straight to morning, but morning would not come around for a long, long time.

28

My mother's voice woke me on the other side of midnight. She had gotten out of bed and was wandering the dark house in search of my father. I pushed off my covers. They seemed extra heavy, like my arms and legs and head. My eyelids would open no more than halfway, and as I went down the hall to the stairs I had to lean against one wall to keep from tipping. I felt like a tree that has been half felled by an ax. I remember thinking that I was sleepwalking, but my brain could not quite finish the word and so the thought came out, *I'm sleepwalk.*

Blue-orange flames danced on the stovetop and cast twisting shadows on the kitchen walls. I turned off the burners and stood there, forgetting in the quiet why I had come downstairs in the first place.

Hinges creaked.

A descending voice called, "John?"

I followed the voice through the living room to the basement door. The first two stairs were dim. The third was dark. Beyond that I could see nothing at all. But that was okay. There was a light bulb at the bottom, and all I had to do was pull the string.

I started down with one hand on the railing. As I lifted my foot from the third step, the railing ended. I was holding onto air . . . and treading onto air. The fourth step had packed up its bags and walked right out of the world. I heard my mother call out one last time, but it was as if her voice had been tied to a fast, noiseless train rushing away down a tunnel. ". . . *John*?" And then silence.

I fell.

Not for long.

Ground caught me. Soft ground, nicely padded down with moss. The moss was warm. So was the air. Warm and humid and teeming with smells. Soil. Salt. Shale or granite. Something else, too. Something out of place that prickled the sensitive skin inside my nose. My mind spun out of orbit and stopped on a scene from my childhood: me at the kitchen table with my mother, sniffing her glass of pinot and telling her, yes, I do believe I'm picking up a hint of blueberries along with earthiness, mushrooms, mmmm, mushrooms, and oooh, my favorite, wet teddy bear. I always gave her one smell that didn't belong in a wine bottle, and when it came to *this* smell, here, now, 'wet teddy bear' wasn't so far off the mark . . . if the teddy bear in question had been wet for a very long time and its fur had grown rank, wild.

I sat up. No matter how hard I tried, I could not convince myself that the mossy ground beneath me was or had ever been in the basement. The basement was concrete, and this was no concrete. I got up slowly and turned around in the dark until I felt sure I was facing the staircase—or the part of it I had walked down before I'd fallen. I had not dropped far, and if I could just find the last stair, I could pull myself out of this place that I had landed and climb back into my house. This thought and nothing else kept me from collapsing into a bunch of useless, quivering pieces. I took two careful steps, my hands outstretched and trembly. I was wide awake now. I had never been more awake in my life. One ragged breath gave way to another. The moss sank beneath my bare feet, getting up between my toes, and at last—but far too late—my search ended. I touched a wall. Its surface was coarse and uneven and damp, but I did not stop to consider what any of that might mean. I reached up for the staircase, up, up, up, and as high as I could reach, there was only that wall. That ridged, slimy, *rock* wall.

I tried to jump, but my knees had locked and refused to bend. I was frozen with my hands up above my head, like someone doing the wave at the ballpark. It came to me on a slanting, sideways logic that if I stood very still and very quiet, if I just *stopped*, everything else might also stop. No more tick-tocking for the clocks, no more movements after this one. My good pal Time and I were calling it quits on this whole silly existence thing. We were exiting ourselves stage left. If the staircase could up and go without even a goodbye, then so could we.

My shoulders began to shake from the exertion of holding up my arms. At the ends of those arms, my hands were pressed to the slick rock wall. As I stood there, attempting to unbecome myself, something large and hairy crawled over my splayed fingers. Something with no feet but many, many legs.

I screamed.

No, that is an understatement.

I became a scream. My body turned into one big, backpedaling, howling throat. The sac around my nuts cinched up like a pouch with a drawstring. Piss gushed down my legs. I screamed and screamed in that dark place that was not the basement of my house, and my screams echoed off the rock walls and cavorted in the moist, bottled air. A cave. I was in a cave, and I was not alone down here . . . I was lost but not alone.

A sound reached me through the racket I was making. A soft, sandpapery hiss like static on an enormous television. It was coming from above me. *Everywhere* above me. I looked up into the seething dark overhead, and now I could hear pieces of that darkness coming detached from the whole, landing with thumps on the ground. These thumps did not stay put where they fell; they hit the moss in a scamper. A fat, squirming weight dropped onto my upturned face and clenched down like a dozen-fingered hand. Prickly hairs scratched my cheeks and stuck into my open mouth. I grabbed the thing to tear it off me. It held on. It was strong. Terror made me stronger. I snapped its legs like celery stalks. I broke them, tore them out, tossed them. Hot juices dripped onto my skin. The mouth part of the thing—the fang part—tickled at my scalp but got caught in my long hair before it could bite into my skull. That it could have done so, I have no doubt. I flung the broken, twitching body away. One of its crooked legs clung stubbornly to my jaw, and I slapped it off.

A strange thing happened then, as I blinked its blood out of my eyes.

An impossible thing.

My vision cleared.

Up above the dark was beginning to crack. A thin, red seam appeared, dividing the black of the cave's walls from the seething black of the cave's roof. The roof was lifting. The roof was not a roof, and the cave was not a cave, and the bloodied light spilling down the rock was not like any light I had ever known. I stood in a ravine, wide and deep and closed off at either end, with a floor covered by vegetation that was as soft as moss and as pale as the fish that live miles under the sea. Above me the roof swayed as it rose. Its surface crawled with tarantulas. Thousands of tarantulas, some as tiny as my thumbnail, others the size of my head, a few so large their limbs could have wrapped around a child. They swarmed over one another, their bodies and legs woven into a furred and scuttering tapestry that offered no glimpse of what lay behind it. Some continued to fall, and those that did dropped from greater and greater heights. One hundred feet. Two hundred. Higher . . . higher. The roof stopped rising. Still I could see nothing on either side of it. From where I stood, far below, it filled the frame of the ravine.

An enormous, deafening BOOM shook the ground. I kept on my feet, somehow, as my bones rattled inside me. The roof slid aside and the sky came into view. It was no sky that had ever looked down on Earth. It was a hazy, swimming red punctured by stars so bright they burned the eyes. A black moon sat low and heavy in its mold. White flowers stirred along the high, rocky cliffs. I smelled salt and decay on the breeze. I pissed again, a weak dribble, the last of my sanity. My mouth hung open. I was drooling. Another BOOM came. Another. Another. BOOM. BOOM. BOOM. Mom had warned me not to step anywhere that was dark, even if it was in my own house, and now—

And now—

And now—

My brain stuttered at the sight of what came next. The sky went away. A head eclipsed it. Eyes like yawning yellow searchlights, with slits for pupils, looked down into the ravine over a snout whose nostrils each could have fit a streetcar. The snout was covered with tangled black fur, and the fur was crawling with tarantulas. Two giant batwing ears perked up curiously—crookedly—atop the creature's shaggy head. It had a dog's friendly face, and a cat's cold intelligent eyes, and when those eyes found me, they widened. It gave two big sniffs that tugged the pajamas up on my body, lifted the hair off my scalp. Its lips parted into a happy grin. A grin full of spiders. The air rushed back out from the tunnels of its nostrils and knocked me down flat onto my rear. The creature's breath was hot and spoiled and so . . . familiar. I had smelled its breath before in the closet of my mother's office, but how could that be? How could *any* of this be?

The dog thing opened its mouth. Its teeth were me sized, dentist sized, and blacker than the glass born inside a volcano. Its gums and jowls were the deep red of overripe plums. The drool that ran from them ran in slow, thick ropes that looked heavy enough to climb. As the dog thing lowered its head, its snout slid into the crack of the ravine and dragged against the walls, stretching its grin wider and wider.

Finally, it stopped.

The crack was too thin. The dog thing's mouth could not reach me, but its tongue was not out of the question. Like a slow pink waterfall, a waterfall of mottled flesh, its tongue spilled down from overhead. I watched as the tip of it swayed closer, then I closed my eyes and watched no more. Too much. Too much. Too much. I hugged myself, sitting there underneath the shadow of that cavernous mouth and the black moon of that red night sky so far away from home. I wrapped my arms around my legs and I hugged myself. And when the hand touched my shoulder, I pulled away from it.

"There you are," said a soft voice, distant and yet close. "Come on now."

I let the hand take my hand and help me to my feet. The hand pulled, and I followed. I opened my eyes for a moment, but there was no one there. There was only my hand out in front of me, afloat. I closed my eyes and carried on, guided through the dark. The air cooled. The moss thinned beneath my soles until I was walking on what felt like hard-packed dirt and then, after a passage of time I cannot measure or make sense of, a passage of time that lasted for a thousand breaths but only a few careful steps, concrete.

"Careful, Dear."

I set my foot down, and gasped when it stopped short. Slowly, I started up the stairs. There seemed a great many of them—far more than I could count. And yet my legs did not ache, my lungs did not burn. I climbed. I climbed. I climbed. A door creaked open, creaked shut. My toes clenched around thick, plush threads. *Carpet.* I was standing in my living room, in Boston, on a chilly night in the middle of March.

My mother took me trembling into her arms and held me.

"It's okay, Mike," she said as I wept into her neck. "It's okay. I found you."

PART THREE
CHANGE

29

After I was done crying and shaking, I put my mother to bed. I wiped off her feet and kissed her on the forehead and tucked her in under the covers. She was already half asleep. "You're a good boy," she said as I turned off the light. Walking down the hall, I could not quite keep to a straight line.

I took a shower. There were prickly black hairs—spider hairs—in my beard. My face looked as if it had been dipped in honey, only this honey was colorless and smelled coppery rather than sweet. I washed off the blood and bits that had stuck to me and watched them run down the drain. When I got out, I carried my urine-soaked pajamas and sweaty t-shirt to the laundry basket in my room. I got dressed. As I sat down to put on socks, I discovered a tiny sliver of pale moss beneath one of my toenails. I started to shake again. I went back to the bathroom and took another shower, this one cold because the hot water had been spent. It was hard to move after because of the shivers, but that was all right. Freezing, I could almost pretend that the warm, wet place beneath my house had been nothing more than a nightmare.

Eventually, I walked down to the basement door. The lights were on in the living room, so I would be able to see the stairs if they were there.

They weren't.

Past the threshold stood a long drop down sheer rock, into that thick, bland moss. My head gave a dizzy whirl, and my hand clutched reflexively at the wall. I was standing at the ravine's edge underneath the sky's churning red cauldron, and if I lifted my eyes just a little, if I let them wander across the chasm, what would I see? What kind of land would I find staring back at me from that terrible unknowable beyond? I shut the door. Hard. Then I saw faint red light seeping through the crack beneath, and ran for the kitchen. I came back with duct tape and sealed the crack. That wasn't good enough, so I sealed the cracks alongside and above the door, too. Oh, but that made a new problem, which was Cassie and the questions she would have if she showed up to find the basement under airtight quarantine. I emptied one of my mother's enormous bookcases, pushed the bookcase in front of the door, and refilled the shelves from top to bottom. Now all the tape was hidden, and I could tell Cassie that my mother had almost tripped down the stairs in the night. Yes, that would work. My mother had almost tripped down the stairs, scaring me badly enough that I had blocked off the basement until I could buy a lock.

For a while I continued to stand there, still seeing that long drop down into that distant bed of moss. Something didn't add up. When walking down into the basement I had fallen only a few feet—or what had felt like a few feet, in the dark—but the drop that waited beyond the door now would have killed me just as surely as a knife to the heart or a bullet to the head. Unless . . . I remembered the stairs. No, that is not quite accurate. I did not remember the stairs themselves but the *feeling* of them. The climb was still in my legs, a memory of movement, like the gentle lasting sway that comes from a day of riding rollercoasters. I had climbed further than I had fallen. I didn't know how it could be possible—I didn't know how any of this could be possible—but I knew it to be true nevertheless. With my mother's hand around mine and her voice guiding me, I had climbed further than I had fallen, and I had returned from wherever I had gone.

My body decided it was time to move again, and spun me around with a jerk. I returned the duct tape to the kitchen, a light sweat standing out on my cheeks and brow. Before I left, I shut the window by the stove. I didn't like the window cracked open like that, and I couldn't remember why I'd left it that way. My mind was hopping. The back and front door had little rubber curbs on the bottom to keep the cold out, and that was good, very good, but there were other cracks. So many cracks and so little time. I went upstairs to the hall closet where I kept my limited collection of tools. I was no handy man, but I could shore up a leaky pipe and change a mean light bulb. I opened the closet carefully, standing back as far as I could, and breathed a sigh of relief to see everything inside and in the right place. On the floor was a bucket of putty that I had used to hide some old nail holes. I took the bucket under one arm and set to work downstairs with a skinny metal spatula. It felt good to work. It felt like the sane thing to do. I filled in cracks on the walls and windowsills. I went from room to room and when I came to the spare room that sat directly over the basement, I made sure to turn the light on and test the floor past the doorway with one foot. The floor was solid. The floor was *there*.

At least on this side.

30

"You sure seem up and at 'em this morning," Cassie said with a touch of resentment. She looked like a whole night's worth of tossing and turning bundled into one shuffling package. Cassie without coffee, proving that the dead really do walk among us. She gave me a kiss that I felt but did not taste. "Big day?"

"Big day," I said, not knowing that it would be my last day, too.

31

I had seen what was on the other side, as Mom had promised I would. There was another world, and it was very far, or it was very close. A world of warm, lasting nights and lush, poisoned life. A hungry world, where things slithered and crawled and giant beasts roamed underneath a wound of a sky.

I had been there.

I had breathed its air.

And I had found my way back. Somehow, I had found my way back. But next time I might not be so fortunate, and I did not doubt there would be a next time unless I could find Tiffany and force her to undo what she'd started before more of my world fell through the cracks . . .

The *growing* cracks.

32

A cold dawn had broken over Boston. Gray clouds sealed off the sun. The light that glowed through them was as icy as the air. I took the train into town, to my normal stop, and then I chased the ghost of my breath around the block until Napkin Guy earned enough change to rent a seat in Dunkin Donuts. I could have gone to him right away, since his spot on Harvard Avenue was behind Mom's corner and anything out of her direct line of sight might as well have been on another planet . . . only I wasn't so sure about her ears. She seemed like the type of person to hear a tissue drop across the city, and I wasn't going to risk my voice reaching her. For all she knew I'd given up my search (or had my search ended for me), and I wanted her to go on thinking that I was out of the picture.

Dunks was a shoebox with two tables, a counter to order at, and a counter for sitting. The air smelled sweet and bitter and greasy all at once. Stepping into the warmth should have felt nice after outside, but it didn't. I skipped thawing out and went straight to sweating inside my coat. Over at the condiment station, Napkin Guy was collecting his napkins. He was a thin man, as white and delicate as the flowers he made. His uncombed sandy hair reached down to his shoulders. He filled out a pair of big checkered sneakers by wearing several wool socks on each foot. I tried to look casual as I ordered from the lady behind the counter, but it was difficult because the display case was full of flies. They frolicked on the bear claws and bathed in the icing, their shimmery green-black bodies moving about busily. The frame of the case was aluminum, but its floor did not sit flush with its walls, and through the cracks came more flies, hopping, buzzing. Was it a happy accident that had brought them here of all places? Or had they sniffed the feast from the other side? I swallowed. Thickly. If smells could slip between this world and their world, what might be smelling *me?*

"Hey," said the woman. "I asked if you wanted any food with that."

"No. No thank you."

Something else gnawed at my brain. Mom said the cracks were getting wider, but were they really? Or was I the one cracking and expanding in some undefinable way, allowing me to see and touch what was already there . . . what had always been there right under the surface?

My coffee mug rattled slightly on its saucer as I walked to the window where Napkin Guy was posted. I took a seat one stool away from him so he wouldn't feel crowded by my presence, and so no one else could sit between us without being sandwiched. If he remembered me from our brief conversation on Monday, he gave no indication. I made a show of minding my business, looking out the window as I sipped my coffee. Really I was watching him from the corner of one eye. He had taken a few straws in addition to his napkins and he used the straws as stems for his flowers. Petals bloomed under the deft, thoughtless motions of his hands. To keep the flowers from coming unraveled at the bottom, he wrapped them in wires, which he then twisted into little human figures, so that the final presentation was that of a miniature person holding up an enormous blossom.

"Those are pretty," I said.

He said nothing.

Across the street a nightmare climbed out of the storm drain. It didn't come out easily. It was almost too big to come out at all. The spider stood as tall as a border collie, except on many more legs and without any hair on its whole body. Its flesh was whiter than the flesh of my thighs and stretched so tight that every movement it made highlighted the flex and twist of cartilage. Two glossy black eyes stuck out prominently above its mouth, which featured a pair of thick, close-set fangs that almost resembled buckteeth.

"Do you make a lot of those?" I asked Napkin Guy uneasily, but he didn't look up from his newest creation.

Mr. Buckteeth scuttled one way, halted, scuttled back. He looked lost. I could sympathize. His eyes swiveled in their ridged seats. And stopped. On me. At least they seemed to— without pupils, they might have been staring the other way or *every* way, for all I knew. I took a deep breath. Mr. Buckteeth couldn't see me. Of course not. Of course not. He scurried across the street, in my direction.

Fear made me bolder.

I reached for the closest paper flower, brought its open bud to my nose, and inhaled deeply, as Mom had done yesterday. "Mmmmmm. Very nice."

"That one's a tulip," Napkin Guy said without looking my way. "It smells like violin strings sound when they make sad music."

I took another sniff. I didn't want to seem insincere. "It really does. How'd you get it to smell like that?"

"I didn't do anything. It was born that way."

Mr. Buckteeth came to my window. He got up on hind legs and pawed at the glass. A red squiggle ran down the skin of his belly, like a single engorged vein. His eyes quivered ever so slightly as they looked up at me. Their black surface showed no reflection, no consciousness.

"What's that one smell like?" I pointed at the lily with a trembling finger.

"Language," said Napkin Guy, "when language is well spoken."

"And that one?" I asked about the flower he was busy nurturing between his hands.

"Don't know. Hasn't bloomed yet."

Mr. Buckteeth let himself down off the window. He walked over to the entry-nook. Pushed on the door. It rattled in its frame, and the lady behind the counter glanced up from her phone. "Stupid draft," she grumbled.

"I bet you get a lot of admirers," I said, trying to keep the edge out of my voice.

"People like my flowers." He stated this as a fact, without pride.

"You ever show them off to anybody?"

"There's Tom, but he don't ever smell them right. He's got a bad nose, and *he* smells bad."

"A good nose is rare. That's what my mother used to say. I bet *somebody* has to smell them right, though."

"Only you and Mom."

I swallowed my excitement. My nerves were zapping like live wires underneath my skin. "Mom?"

"Yeah. Mom. She sits on the corner and she don't ever move."

"That's a funny nickname," I said as Mr. Buckteeth scratched and shoved at the door. The lady stepped out from behind the counter with an irritated sigh. "She must have a lot of kids, Mom."

"We're all her kids. That's what she says."

The lady walked up to the door. She started to pull it open and I stuck out a foot to press it shut. "It's cold," I said. "Don't let the cold in. Please."

"I was just going to fix the thing," she said, looking very much like she wanted to fix me too while she was at it.

"I'll hold it shut." I could feel Mr. Buckteeth pushing to come in and say hello . . . perhaps share a bite.

The lady huffed off.

This interaction didn't seem to register with Napkin Guy, who had begun the process of budding his new flower.

"Mom sounds like a sweet woman. I bet you don't call her Mom, though, since you two are so close. I bet you use her name."

"Mom is her name."

I dug my fingers into my thighs and laughed a high, cracky laugh. "Mom can't be her *real* name."

"Sure it can. It's just short. Like Dick for Richard or Betsy for Elizabeth."

"What's Mom short for?"

"Mother."

Jesus. Fuck. "That's it?"

"Part of it."

"What's the other part?" I said, making blank eye contact with my hopeful guest outside the door.

"Mary."

"Mother Mary," I repeated, not really hearing.

"Yeah. She used to be Mother Mary, until everyone got lazier and lazier and she just became Mom. She's real famous. She was in the Globe, but they got it all wrong, she said. They talked about her like she was cuckoo, but they were only making funny of what would have scared them too much to believe." Napkin Guy tweaked open the last petal of his flower. He sniffed and then wrinkled his nose. "This one smells like dying. Here. You have it."

He set the white rose in my hand, and at that moment there came a strong push on the door. A tremendous, *monstrous* push, as if Mr. Buckteeth had grown as large as a buffalo. I gasped as my foot was shoved back and wind sliced into the coffee shop. A man walked in wearing a thick yellow construction jacket and an equally thick Boston accent. "Hey, buddy, get your leg out of the way. What's the matter with you? You think you own the place?"

The man wasn't alone. He had picked up a passenger.

Mr. Buckteeth clambered off his back and plopped to the floor. One crooked, bony limb brushed my ankle. I hopped up onto my stool, both feet planted in a gargoyle's crouch, then I lunged for the closing doorway. The man swore in surprise as I shouldered past him. A second later he shouted, "Hey, guy, you left your coat!"

I didn't care.

I ran down the sidewalk, death rose in hand.

33

Mr. Buckteeth had singled me out. As food or for camaraderie, I didn't know, but he had pinpointed me from across the street, and that could only mean I was different to him than everyone else. Maybe I smelled or gave off a shimmer, or maybe he simply saw me seeing him, and that recognition was enough. Rattling the door proved that he could interact with the world to an extent. He could also be killed by anything on Earth, like the maggots that the boy in the park had crushed unwittingly beneath his shoes, but there was a line drawn somewhere, a crack that he could not completely cross. The man who had come into the coffee shop . . . Mr. Buckteeth had been able to hitchhike on him, but could he have done more? Could he have sunken his two goofy fangs into the soft of the man's throat? I don't think so. I think his deepest bite would have made little more than a tickle, a feeling for the man as if he had been stung by a mosquito. And I think that if the man had slapped at Mr. Buckteeth, the poor spider would have caved as easily as a paper flower, leaving the man to wipe off his hand with a sensation of stickiness that would soon be forgotten. Because Mr. Buckteeth wasn't all the way *here*. He was a ghost from another world, something more and something less than a shadow, waiting to be thrown and scattered off the face of existence. He could scratch at the window and knock on the door, but he could not let himself inside.

He did not belong to Earth.

And if *he* didn't, did I?

34

All that I didn't dwell on until later. After my escape from Dunkin Donuts, my thoughts were swimming about far too fast to single out and catch. I ran myself ragged before I stopped to consider what I was going to do next. Napkin Guy's white rose had wilted from getting shaken about in my hand. It was good and dead. I gave it over to the wind, then I walked on with my head down until I caught my breath.

Mother Mary, Mother Mary. As far as leads went, it was a pretty thin ledge to hang onto, but Napkin Guy had given me a teeny bit more than just a nickname. He had hinted at some context, some history, as well. According to Mom, she had been in the newspapers, and I was inclined to believe that was true seeing as she hadn't told me one lie yet as far as I could tell. The Globe had written her off as crazy, but when? And for what?

I tried an internet search but my phone was dying, so I started downtown to the library. I'd want a computer anyway if I was going to do any real digging. How did Mom charge *her* phone? I wondered as I walked, though I had a pretty good idea. There'd been a wall socket next to Napkin Guy. He already paid for her food . . . why not give her cell a zap too? The realization flooded my mouth with saliva. For the first time since yesterday, I felt hungry. If Napkin Guy borrowed her phone, perhaps I could borrow her phone from Napkin Guy and find the number to a certain someone in the contact's list. But what would I say? What could I possibly tell Tiffany to keep her on the line once she heard my voice? Unless I texted her pretending to be Mom . . . no. If Mom wasn't the type to text (and I had a strong suspicion she wasn't), then a text sent from Mom's number would raise all kinds of red flags and who could say if her daughter would even respond?

For much of the walk I was lost inside my head, hardly aware of my surroundings. But after a while I resurfaced, and once I did, I was unable to go back under again.

The city had changed.

Mushroomy drafts rose out of sewer grates. Manhole covers leaked buttered red light onto pedestrians. In

Kenmore Square, flies covered an entire building. The sound of them was a heavy drone, like traffic on a freeway. All light from inside was blocked out by the moving curtains of their bodies. People passing by the building gave a shiver or walked a little faster. Drinking fountains sprayed tiny squirming larvae into open mouths. Cracks in the sidewalk sprouted thorned weeds that bled black sap whenever stepped on or kicked. I passed a church whose stained glass window was completely dark, and whose doors, when they opened, looked in on a field of tall pale grass that swayed in starlit dew, stretching far beyond the back wall of the church. The people walking through those doors became silhouettes the moment they stepped across the threshold, and a little while later they were gone, lost in the grass. Somewhere they would be settling into their pews, opening their bibles, singing their hymns, but that somewhere was nowhere I could visit anymore.

It had fallen through the cracks.

35

The library remained the library, and thank God for that. Thank Jesus and Mother Mary too, while we're at it. I all but dived through the doors as soon as I saw the lobby and the bookcases waiting in the huge room past the stairs.

I found a computer. The internet required a library card to use, and I had one of those—this place had been my mother's church while growing up, and she had made sure to baptize me at an early age. My hands were sweaty, but my bad finger had stopped throbbing. The swelling had gone down as well. I'd been too preoccupied with big changes to notice such a little one, but there it was, getting better while everything else was coming unhinged. And I'll be honest. It scared me. Worse than my walk across town. My finger beginning to heal now of all times seemed the opposite of a good sign. It seemed an omen. It did not say that whatever infection had been given to me was passing through my system . . . it said that the infection was settling in, putting up walls and planting crops, getting nice and comfortable in its new home.

I pulled up the website for the Boston Globe. Their archives dated back to 1872 and in recent years had been digitized for easy public consumption. All they asked for was a subscription or a meager one-time flat payment. I debated my options for a moment and then laughed out loud, a huge barking laugh that turned several heads my direction. Here I was, straddling Earth and an alien world that wanted to swallow me whole, and I was still pinching pennies. I took out my debit card and signed myself up for the lifetime pass. If the Globe could lead me to Tiffany, and Tiffany could put *my* globe back into orbit, I'd have my subscription printed out, laminated, and framed on the wall above my bed.

"Don't get your hopes up," I mumbled, but I couldn't help it. My hopes had had so very little to feed on these past few days that a nibble felt like a full meal to them. I typed 'Mother Mary' into the search function. Predictably, the keyword turned up a slew of articles related to Catholicism and the church. One hundred and eleven pages' worth, to be exact. Good old puritanical Boston. I skimmed through the headlines. Halfway through my eyes started to gloss over. At last they snagged on something, a detail so tiny I only recognized it at a subconscious level. The title of the article was <u>Woman in Sixties Gives Birth to Girl,</u> and the preview of the first lines read:

Marianne Louise became a new mother today at age 63, making her one of the oldest women on record to give birth, but claims of immaculate conception are causing the bigger stir for this 'Mother Mary.'

'Mother Mary.' Were it not for those two tiny quotation marks, I might have passed right over the article. But those quotation marks implied a nickname, and that was enough to hook me. The rest dragged me deeper.

Born to Jacob and Sarah Munro, both schoolteachers, Marianne carried on the family profession at Heritage Elementary, where she taught kindergarten. After her husband's untimely death left her a widow in her early twenties, she remained unattached and childless for almost thirty years. "I never needed any children," she told us during our interview. "My kids are my children. I've had hundreds of them. How could I wish for any more?" Wishes or not, Marianne received last April when she discovered she was pregnant. Asked about the father, Marianne insisted she had been with no other man since her late husband. She continues to maintain this stance of celibacy despite backlash from the Catholic Church, who initially declared her late conception a 'miracle' but went on to quietly retract their statement. Archbishop Theodore Griffith offered no further comment on the matter except to remind his community that "there is only one Mother Mary and to attach her name to another would be an affront to the Son." Marianne lives in Cambridge. Her daughter remains unnamed.

"Fuck," I said. Loudly. "Sorry, sorry."

I was about to back out of the article when I noticed the date. January 14th, 1957. That made Marianne Louise, if she was indeed the Mom of Beacon Corner, almost one hundred and twenty years old. It also put Mom's unnamed daughter in her late fifties. I licked the inside of my gums, where Tiffany's secret tooth had hidden. She had looked so young . . . but then her mouth had looked so normal.

On the outside.

I laughed under my breath. And to think I had been worried about pushing the limits of my pediatrics' specialization by seeing her. If only I had known.

I paused.

Did I really believe that a woman born in the nineteenth century was sitting on the corner of Beacon, and that her daughter, who predated the Vietnam War, didn't even look old enough to buy a beer?

Yes. Yes, I did. After what I'd seen this week, I'd believe in the Easter Bunny if someone showed me a big enough egg.

I typed 'Marianne Louise' into the search bar. This time only three articles came up. The first I had already read. The second was dated one year later, in 1958: 'Mother Mary'

<u>Burns down House</u>. Eager to get to the meat, I skimmed the initial sentences recapping Marianne's fifteen minutes of fame and ensuing notoriety. On a snowy night in February, Marianne saturated the first floor of her house in gasoline and set it ablaze. She then went outside and told the firefighters who arrived that her daughter was still inside 'with the spiders.' They found the baby girl upstairs in her crib, sleeping soundly in a room full of smoke. Jason Belkin, one of the firefighters, said he didn't know how the girl survived. He called it a miracle. Meanwhile, a raving Marianne fought all attempts to be moved inside out of the cold because inside, she said, she would be trapped with 'them.' She was taken into custody. Her daughter, Abigail Louis, was passed along to social services.

"Abigail," I said. "Found you, you bitch. Found you."

The third article was only a paragraph long and must have been tucked somewhere far back in the newspaper when it was published later that fall. It briefly recounted Mom's pregnancy and breakdown before going on to inform that she had been declared unsound of mind and sent to Harbrook Hill, a mental hospital in northern Massachusetts.

"But you got out, didn't you? You got out, and you came back to Boston, and after a while everyone forgot about you and your daughter." A man shh'ed me. I shh'ed him back. "Where did she go? Where did little Abigail go?"

I searched for 'Abigail Louise' on the off chance she'd made another appearance in the Globe after the state adopted her. No luck. It was time to broaden my horizons. Armed with the full names of both mother and daughter, I attacked the vast body of the internet. Thoughts about the possible father, Mom's fear of indoors, and young Abigail's improbable survival in a smoky room were pushed to the back of my mind. I could ask all the questions I wanted to later when I found Abigail. Until then everything else was a distraction.

I knew the name of the school that Marianne had taught at, but the district that the school belonged to had shut down in the early eighties and so that proved a dead end. I dug up the number for Harbrook Hill and used the last remaining sliver of life on my phone to call the institution. They confirmed that a Marianne Louise had been admitted in 1958 and discharged in 1964, but patient records were sealed and nothing more could be said. Further poking around led me to a list of late-life conceptions on Wikipedia, where Marianne's name popped up again. For the last time. Her moment in the spotlight had occurred before the internet was around to memorialize her, and as a result she had disappeared the instant the public turned its eye away. I tracked down her birth records using her maiden name and year of birth, which I calculated by counting backward from her age at the time of the first Globe article. There were no death records to go along with them. Of course there weren't. I shifted my search to her daughter, with no success whatsoever. Abigail Munro, born on January 14th, 1957, was a nonentity; she dropped into foster care and never surfaced again.

I rubbed my eyes with the heels of my hands. Noon was in sight, and the library was getting busy. Footsteps thumped around on the floor overhead. It sounded as if there were a convention taking place up there, or a middle school dance minus the music. For the next few hours I hunted every corner of the web that came to mind. I pulled up the profiles of each Abigail Louise on Facebook, Instagram, LinkedIn, not to mention a few dating websites. I tried Abby, Abbey, Abi, even Ab, and I found no one remotely resembling the girl who had strolled into my office on Monday. But was that such a surprise? Baby Abigail was almost sixty years old. She could have been a grandma, and grandmas didn't often take to social media.

My forehead found its way to the desk. I was thirsty, tired, and shaky from spent adrenaline. This wasn't how the search was supposed to go. Diligence was meant to be rewarded. Study hard, pass the test. Dig deep, strike oil. Water at the very least. *Something* to slake your thirst. It wasn't fair that I could uncover so much and still know so little. Who was to say Abigail was even the girl's name anymore? She'd been separated from her mother at one year old, all but orphaned, and since then she had lived two of my lives, found and bonded with that same mother, and still, *still*, she wore a face that could pass for a child's. Abigail Louise, sometimes known as Tiffany, was a gulf that grew wider the more I searched for the other side.

Hopeless.

It was hopeless.

My neighbor had fallen asleep with his head back and his jaws wide. Flies buzzed inside his open mouth. He looked as though he were gargling them except for his closed eyes. I regarded him without surprise, without disgust. I regarded him and felt nothing at all. Upstairs the noise of the convention had grown soft. Footsteps continued to thump around, but the feet in question might have been miles away. I picked up my things to leave.

Outside I looked back at the library.

Every window above the first floor had gone dark, with a tint of red and a suggestion of starlight.

36

I didn't know what to do or where to go so I headed home. The green line was packed with tourists, while the red was a cattle car of people leaving work. I found one of the last open seats and waited as the train carried me underground. Between Park and South Station the windows looked out on stone walls. After South Station, the walls vanished. They smoothed out and darkened until there was nothing there, and from that nothing a night sky was born, its skin a red, squalling red, rashed by thousands of stars. To the east fog swirled in ribbons through a rocky wasteland. Crags jutted over deep, twisting ravines. Black hillsides sprouted deathly white flowers. No birds flew. Nothing walked unless it walked too low to be seen. The horizon bled down onto loneliness and despair.

Behind me, to the west, rock gave way to fields of pale grass as tall and thick as corn. Flies swarmed the air in patchy clouds. Here and there an enormous white-bone tree held out thick, outstretched arms, and I thought back to the AMC by the Common, the crucifix shape that I had witnessed in the movie theater . . . and the slow, scaly, *scraping* movement of whatever had been wrapped around it in the dark. Past the fields was a looming shadow that made the night look bright by comparison. A forest to mock the forests of Earth, with trees like skyscrapers and leaves like sailboats riding among the stars. I could not see the edge of the forest in either direction, and I could not imagine where it ended, if it ever did.

The operator's voice called out, *"Broadway,"* then the train stopped and the doors slid open on utter, deep-sea silence. The passengers getting off appeared to float, as the train did not quite sit level on this strange world. They faded with each step and soon were gone. Those boarding approached as smoky shadows that became solid as they passed over the threshold. Normal people, going about normal lives, melting into and out of existence against a landscape they could not see or touch or smell. A landscape that for them was not there.

When the train surfaced from underground, I nearly sobbed to find my world waiting on the other side.

37

I came home ready to tell Cassie I wasn't feeling well and didn't want to get her sick. Anything to send her on her way without making her worry. But I didn't need to say a thing. Her morning fatigue had hatched into a fever. She had a distant, shell-shocked look. The 'her' in her eyes had stepped out from behind the wheel and moved to the backseat. She didn't ask about my missing coat or even seem to notice I was back early, so I dropped my story and told her to go get some rest. She asked if I was sure. I said I was. She stopped at the door to tell me she hadn't even started dinner yet, and I gave her a kiss on the mouth to shut her up. If that sounds romantic, it wasn't. I wanted her gone.

"It's supposed to clear up tomorrow," she said. "I was hoping the three of us could go for a little road trip to Salem. Stroll the town. It's been so long since your mom's gotten out of the house, *really* gotten out of the house. We have our walks, you know, but I just thought it would have been nice to go somewhere all together."

"Yeah," I said. "It would have."

I locked the door behind her. I tucked the key back into my shirt. Then I lay face down on the carpet, clutched onto the threads with both hands, and breathed in the dust that had gathered there over the years. The dust of myself, of my family, of my home on this cracking windowpane called Earth.

38

I spent the evening tending to basic chores—dinner, laundry, dishes—clinging onto the last thin string that connected me to what had been my life. Underneath my movements I was very still, like the water at the bottom of a well. I was drawing something from deep within myself, something cold and heavy that strained the ropes of my bucket. I had to be slow, careful, or the ropes would break and the bucket would fall. Part of me wanted that to happen, was scared of what I would find inside it, hauled from the dark chilly waters that slept at my bedrock, but I kept on pulling, pulling, pulling . . .

Outside the sun had gone down behind the clouds, and the night was starless, moonless, complete. Not a single crack marked its surface. I carried my mother to bed from the couch where she had fallen asleep. I went to the bathroom, trimmed my beard ready for a razor, and shaved my face smooth. My cheekbones and jawbones were high ridges set around deep valleys. I did not recognize myself. That was good. That meant no one else would recognize me either.

My mother got up and turned on the stovetop. I turned it off and returned her to bed.

In the back of her closet was a large cardboard box that had not been opened in years. The clothes inside were moth eaten and much too large for me. I carried the box down the hall to my room. There I pulled a pair of faded blue jeans on over my slacks and buttoned a plaid shirt over the shirt I was already wearing. It occurred to me as I did that Tiffany might have done the same before visiting my office, that her homelessness might have been a sham to throw me off or send me a message. To say, "I am my mother's daughter. I come dressed in her image with a handful of bills and a smile to show you." I put on a leather belt with a big brass buckle, brown leather shitkicker boots, and a matching coat. Last of all I took out my father's cowboy hat. Its wide rim was creased, and its top was dented. I had not worn it since I was a child, since his proposal to my mother, but tonight I had no engagement ring tied to my hair. I had nothing to hide but me.

"I'm sorry, Dad," I said as I put on the hat.

On the way downstairs, I paused outside my mother's room to tell her goodbye but continued without saying a word. I did not want to wake her. Before leaving the house and locking the door behind me, I stopped in the kitchen for duct tape and one of the knives hanging over the sink.

The bucket was almost out of the well. I could see inside it now.

It was filled with coins.

With change.

39

I was never going to find Abigail with my nose to the ground. The trail had gone cold, had been cold from the beginning, and following what little there was to follow had been a waste of time. Which I did not have. Not anymore.

Dawn was hours away, but the sky had begun to brighten. Warm red light seeped through the clouds like blood through cotton and dripped over the dark city. Buildings were coated by it. Street lamps were dimmed. Boston lay sound asleep under two nights, one of them dying while the other, hidden from view, awakened behind thick curtains.

The cab dropped me off in Allston, and I walked from there, bundled against the cold in my dad's leather jacket. His hat shaded my face. His boot heels clocked on the ground. If I was ever going to find Abigail, it would be now, and it would be done the same way I had found her the first time.

Through her love for her mother.

40

All was still at the intersection, including the lump of blankets beneath the marquis. Headlights glimmered down Beacon, but they turned a few blocks away and slipped out of sight. No other cars could be seen in either direction but for those parked silently at the curb. Music played somewhere, a grinding thump-thump-thump of dubstep muffled behind walls. The sound was like gnashing teeth, and it was the only sound there was.

I crossed the street from my corner to her corner. She did not see me coming. Her eyes were closed.

I opened them.

"Marianne."

She looked up at me from her blankets. Her pupils were tinged pink by the dawning red night. They widened in confusion. The confusion turned to recognition.

"You're still here," she said.

"I'm still here," I said, and kicked her in the face. Her nose crunched under my boot heel. The back of her head cracked loudly against the brick wall. She moaned. I kicked her again. She became quiet.

41

Mom sat there as still as she always sat there except for the blood dribbling over her lips. Her right eye was open. Her left had tried to close and gotten stuck halfway. I could not hear her breathing, but I could see her breaths on the iced air. I felt cold. I was cold.

Kneeling, I unwrapped her blankets. The body underneath was wasted down to the bone, with wrinkles so deep they looked like cracks. There were dead flies gathered along the collar of her shirt. Her breasts had burrowed back into her, leaving behind two empty pouches. Everywhere her skin showed there were pockmarks, shades darker than the surrounding flesh, as if she'd suffered from some advanced form of acne that had left no part of her untouched below the neck.

I found her phone tucked between her starved legs. An old flip model. I blinked as an unsettling thought came to me.

What if the device was locked? Wouldn't that be something? To hold Abigail in my hand and find her out of reach behind a four-digit password? But the phone wasn't locked, and the last dialed name, the only dialed name, wasn't Abigail.

It was Tiffany.

I laughed through my nose. So Mom *had* lied at least once, after all. She'd said Tiffany wasn't her daughter's name, and yet it was the name she used for her daughter. These days, anyway. Perhaps she had also lied when she said there was nothing that could be done to help me. I pressed the call button. I'd barely raised the phone to my ear when the ringing stopped with a click and a half-awake voice said, "Mom?"

Tiffany must have been a light sleeper to pick up so fast, but that didn't surprise me. I'd have slept light too if my mother was living out on the street.

"Mom, are you there? Is everything okay?"

"Everything's got a price," I said.

There was a pause. When Tiffany spoke again, she did not sound even a little bit tired. "You. What did you do?"

"I came by to kick her cup of change, but she must have put it away for the night. So I kicked her face instead."

She swallowed something. A sob, maybe. "You motherfucker."

"She's in pretty bad shape," I went on. "I'd recommend an ambulance, but there's some funny looking lumps in her mouth that might get the doctors asking questions. Imagine what would happen if they found out that Miss Marianne Louise wasn't dead but still kicking around at 122 years old.

Why, I don't think they'd *ever* let her out again. I think they'd make her up a nice little room where they could watch her, and that would be such a shame, seeing as she doesn't like it inside, does she?"

"I'll kill you."

"You already did. I'm just having fun with what's left."

I hung up the phone, turned it off so it couldn't ring, and tucked it back between Mom's legs. I had no use for it anymore. Mom's left pupil gave a lazy see-saw roll beneath its half-shut eyelid. I bundled her up and set her straight. After a second's consideration, I fluffed the blanket so that it covered her broken nose in case someone happened by the corner. Well, someone other than her daughter, who I expected to be making a visit very soon. I looked down at the old woman for a moment to see what I felt.

I was still looking after I turned away.

I walked up Beacon toward my office and made a home in the dark underneath a balcony. Then I waited.

42

The clouds marbled as the sky behind them grew brighter. Overhead everything was pastel red with streaks of puce and whorls of scarlet. Shadows crawled away from the light blushing down onto the city, and my gaze followed one of these shadows across the street to the gutter.

A familiar face peered out at me from the storm drain. Blank, black eyes. Two long fangs set too close together.

Mr. Buckteeth had survived his first day on Earth, and it must have been a lonely day because he sure looked happy to see me. He wiggled out of his hidey-hole and came across Beacon high up on his legs like a walking head scratcher, the kind that clutches its wiry limbs to your skull.

I couldn't run, but not because I'd frozen in place. Tiffany was on the way, and I couldn't risk missing her. Missing her would have spelled the end of me just as surely as Mr. Buckteeth's kiss. I did not doubt he could bite me. He was real to me, and I was real to him. We had both stepped between worlds, or fallen through the cracks as Mom might have said, and in some way I still don't completely understand—even now—that made us kin.

With running off the table, I could try to kill him. Stomp him to pieces beneath the same boot heel I used to put down Mom. But suppose Tiffany arrived and saw me before I finished? I'd never get close to her then, and this was all assuming I'd come out the winner of the contest. About *that* I had plenty of doubts. Mr. Buckteeth's fangs might have been goofy, but I'd be willing to bet they worked just fine.

Maybe I'm being too kind on myself, implying I had a single thought in the moment it took him to cross the street, or that I made a decision—any decision—at all. Maybe I *did* freeze, and that was all there was to it.

I backed flat against the wall and stood there, stiffer than a body in a coffin. Mr. Buckteeth scuttled up onto the curb. His hairless body was the color of bubblegum in the strange light spilling down over Boston. He joined me under the balcony, and after that I saw only his silhouette, crooked, spindly, quick. I held my breath. I fixed my eyes to a lamppost across the street. The manic tap-tap-tap of his approach slowed. Stopped. Nothing happened for so long that I began to wonder if he'd lost interest in me. Then a sharp tip, like a splinter, dug itself into my right calf. Another tip dug into my left thigh as Mr. Buckteeth climbed me on legs as crude as stakes. Every step he took punctured my skin—and I was wearing not one but *two* pairs of pants. He walked up my belly and onto my chest. He stopped. His weight tugged on my father's leather jacket. It was a considering weight. A thoughtful weight. The length of his fangs, smooth and slightly wet, nuzzled into my neck. His shiny black eyes stared up at me; I felt them just below my line of vision, searching, searching, searching . . .

Mr. Buckteeth crawled over my shoulder onto the wall, and continued in a rapid crab shuffle. I heard him tip-tapping across the balcony, and where he went from there, I do not know, for I never saw him again.

My breath came out of me and kept coming until I was completely empty. I touched my body in the dark. There were tiny holes in my clothes, and I was bleeding in half a dozen places. But I was not bitten. I'd learned something as well.

I'd learned why Mom kept so still on her corner, why she never turned her head or lifted a hand except to eat and use the phone.

She kept still to remain unseen.

She kept still so the things that came out of the cracks could not find her.

43

This revelation about Mom, as small as it might have seemed next to what I had uncovered at the library, set my mind into furious motion. I stood there, in the dark of the balcony underneath the clouded red sky, questioning everything that I knew about her—or believed I'd known. I thought of her munching on her sandwich with no apparent hunger, eating as if the very act was a chore, and I asked myself if she ate because she needed to . . . or if she ate to maintain appearances. Nibble through a meal once a day in plain sight, and let people assume the rest. People are great assumers. We make assumptions all the time without even realizing we're making them. Take me, for instance. For all my hours of watching the old woman on the corner, despite not once seeing her on her feet, I'd never stopped to wonder when she got up to stretch her legs or relieve herself. I didn't consider that she might never do those things at all.

I had no more time to wonder now.

A Honda Civic pulled up to the corner, and my oldest, biggest assumption, that Tiffany was homeless, was dispelled once and for all as she got out of the car.

44

She fell out of the driver's seat but caught herself against the door. Leaving it open, she staggered around the car in fuzzy blue slippers. Those slippers looked as though they'd keep her feet nice and warm, but the rest of her, dressed in thin pajama bottoms and an over-sized t-shirt, had no place being out on a bitter night like this. Her hair was undone. With nothing to hold it in check, it scattered every which way as she ran. I still cannot recall the color of it, but I can tell you that her face was just as smooth and tight as ever—even without a ponytail. She had something else, something better, giving her a facelift now.

Fear.

"*Mom*," she said, coming up onto the curb, where she almost fell over again. She continued on as if the world were wobbly under her feet. Maybe it was. The world was anything but reliable these days. I watched her bend down slowly and touch the lump under the marquis—"Mom? Mom?"—and then rise again much faster to run back to her car. She opened the back door. At this point she paused to glance around Beacon suspiciously. Her eyes passed over me. I was standing in the dark, and for her the night was just an ordinary night, lit by a few street lamps and the faint orange city-glow trapped beneath the clouds. There was no special illumination in *her* Boston.

Tiffany returned to Mom, and I stepped out from the balcony and strolled down the sidewalk. My body felt loose and constricted at the same time. My legs couldn't decide if they wanted to fall off at the hip or lock at the knees. Tiffany scooped Mom up in her blankets and started back for the car. I was a dozen feet away and in plain sight. She was going to see me.

"Ma'am!" I called out in a bad Texan drawl. "Is everything okay?"

Tiffany looked at me, but her gaze didn't stick. Without my beard I was just a smooth face underneath a cowboy hat. She slid her mom into the backseat and shut the door. "Everything's fine, don't worry."

"That lady hurt?"

"She's just sick. She's my Grandma. It's okay, really, don't worry. I'll take care of her." All this she tossed over her shoulder without a second glance my direction. She hopped into the driver's seat. As she did, I popped open the back door that she had closed a moment ago. I climbed inside. It was an awkward fit, her mother's legs being on the seat already. I pulled the kitchen knife from my leather coat. I yanked Mom's head up by her wispy gray hair and stuck the edge to her throat.

"All right, Tiffany. Let's see where you live. I've had enough of this corner to last me a lifetime."

45

Tiffany eased down the emergency brake and turned the car onto Harvard Avenue. A few sleeping bags lay snug by Dunkin Donuts. I wondered if Napkin Guy was tucked inside one of them, if he was dreaming of flowers.

"What do you want?" Tiffany said finally.

"To talk."

"I've got nothing to say to you."

"You'll think of something if you don't want to play catch with your mom's head."

"You *fuck.*" Her eyes, cold, bright, stabbed me from the rearview mirror.

"I know. Watch the road."

Mom's legs made for an uncomfortable seat. I sat up and pushed them onto the floor, then I put the knife back to her throat. Blood dripped from her broken nose onto the upholstery. Abrupt pauses interrupted her breaths. She stank like the stuffing in an old couch, one that's sat on the street for a long time in the rain, waiting for the garbage man. A fly wriggled out of her ear and buzzed merrily to her daughter.

Tiffany's hands stayed on the wheel.

"Want me to shoo that for you?" I said.

"What?"

Interesting. If Tiffany couldn't see the fly, that meant even the littlest of cracks had not opened for her. Unless she was playing dumb. She did like games, after all. I wouldn't forget that again.

We'd looped around and passed back over Beacon, headed north down a side street near the spot where I lived with my last girlfriend. A few punks loitered on a stoop. They looked quite picturesque with their studded belts and safety-pinned jackets simmering under the violent night sky. We crossed over a fenced bridge. The scarce traffic moving below us shined headlights onto a highway whose shadows had all boiled away. Its asphalt looked ruddy, soft, ready to be chewed up and spit out in chunks by the tires grinding at it.

"We almost there?"

"Why?" said Tiffany. "Something making you nervous?"

"Yes. Very. In fact, my hands are starting to shake." I moved the knife on Mom's throat. Tiffany became more liberal with the gas.

We entered that queer gray area known both as Upper Allston and Lower Brighton. Quiet suburban streets. Pinched apartments. A few trees here and there, waiting to put on leaves. It hit me then that I might not see spring, that I'd gone through all of winter only to fall a step short of the sun.

"I don't deserve this." My voice had a crack in it. "What you did to me. I didn't earn it. Not even close."

Tiffany said nothing, and that said enough.

She stopped the car in front of a three-story building. Paneled walls cascading like closed blinds. Windows giving back a soft red light.

"This is how we're going to do it," I said. "You'll go first, and I'll carry your old lady. Her blankets will cover up my hands so you won't be able to see my knife, but I don't want you to doubt for a second it's there. If we run into anyone in the stairwell, I'm your boyfriend, and your mom—she'll be good and covered up too—is my sleeping daughter. God knows she's small enough. Do you follow me?"

"No," she said. "I go first."

I nodded. "Good."

We got out of the car and walked up the concrete steps to the stairwell. My mom was light, but Tiffany's mom could have been packed into a FedEx box and shipped without an overweight fee. If I hadn't wrapped her in the blankets myself, I wouldn't have believed I was carrying anything but bones.

"What floor?"

"Top."

That figured. "I hope you live alone."

"I do. I don't get along well with people."

"That's hard to believe. You've got such a nice smile."

"Thanks. Perhaps I'll show it to you again before the night's done."

We climbed the rest of the way in silence. At last she took out a key and wiggled it in a stubborn lock. I paused as she went inside. "Turn on the lights. I want to see where I'm walking."

Tiffany hit a switch on the wall. Hearing that click, seeing her apartment appear, was worth all six flights of stairs. She lived in a one bedroom with a single hallway that connected everything. I had her open all the doors and leave them open except for the door to what must have been the bathroom. That one I told her to leave closed.

Buttery red light leaked from the cracks in its frame.

When I was sure of our privacy, I made Tiffany drag a chair from the dinner table into the living room and then I sat down on the couch with Mom. Those two furnishings—

the table and couch—were all Tiffany had in the whole place, not counting her twin mattress. The tiny amount of clothes she owned hung in her closet. She had no bookcases, no coffee stands, no television. Nor were there any posters or picture frames. Her home was about as homey as Mom's corner on Beacon.

"You're not much of a consumer, are you?"

"I move around a lot."

"Why's that?"

Her jaws tightened. I loosened them by nicking the skin near her mother's windpipe. An easy thing to do, as her mother's skin was thinner than giftwrap.

"Because," Tiffany said, "the dreams get bad when I stick in one place too long."

"What dreams?"

"You going to tell me what to do with this chair?" She knocked its wooden legs on the floor.

"You're a smart girl. You figure it out."

She took a seat. I tossed the roll of duct tape to her.

"Fuck that," she said.

"You want me to take the knife off your old lady, don't you? Do one arm and I'll do the other. Be generous, too. I don't want to see any skin between your elbow and wrist."

Tiffany laid her forearm flat to the arm of the chair. She did a clumsy job of it, having to let go and grab and let go of the roll on every loop, but she didn't do a half-assed job. "Happy?"

"I could piss sunshine. But my mood swings are ugly these days, so lay down that other arm and don't move until I'm done with it. Or who knows what might happen."

She did as I asked, but her eyes did not once leave my face as I used the rest of the duct tape on her. "There," I said, tucking the knife back into my coat, "now we can talk nicely. Please don't forget about it and make me take it out again."

"I've got a good memory."

"I'll bet you do. How far does it go back? The sixties?"

Her head tilted. Not in surprise but in amusement. "You've been poking around."

I lifted the finger that had until recently been as fat as a Merguez sausage. "You gave me a reason to."

"You brought it on yourself."

"Did I?" I said. "You know, that day, I went back to look for your mom. Before you came to my office. I went back to her corner to apologize and give her some money because I felt bad. But she wasn't there. She'd already gone to you." I swallowed. "I've made some pretty big assumptions, but the one you made about me, about the kind of person I was, that assumption beats all."

Tiffany's face had softened, and her eyes had lost their cold sheen. She looked in that moment both as old as she truly was and as young as I had first imagined her to be. An uncertain child. A wearied adult. Her gaze slid to the woman lying next to me on the couch, and she swallowed as I had swallowed.

Bitterly.

"You felt bad?" She laughed, a sound like rocks grinding deep in her throat. "You have no idea what *bad* feels like. No idea at all. People like you, you step on dog shit and your day is ruined. You stub a toe and act like you lost a foot. Miss a night of sleep and call in sick because working would just be too *hard*. But you don't know what hard is. You can't possibly imagine."

"I think I could hazard a guess. After the week I've had."

"No. That's where you're naive, Doctor. You've had but a sip." Tiffany's hands worked into fists. "My mom used to be a teacher. You probably know that from your digging, but did you know she went to church? She was a good little Catholic girl even in her sixties. Then it happened. She got pregnant with me, and the church, her only family she had left, shunned her. They didn't believe what she said about there being no father. They thought she was lying to cover up her sin. You see, she wasn't married, and unwed women aren't supposed to find themselves *with child*, no matter their age. So they pushed her out like she later pushed me out, and left her all alone to raise the little miracle who had come uninvited into the world."

"Uninvited."

"Yes," Tiffany said. "No welcome mat had been laid out for me, but there I was anyway. *What* I was, though, was a different matter. Something had changed inside her, having me in her belly . . . something had cracked. Soon our house was busy with all sorts of unwanted guests. So was her classroom. And the kids in her classroom. Everywhere she went they were there, and only for her. Until one day she couldn't take it anymore."

"She set fire to the house," I said, "with you inside."

"She wasn't trying to kill me if that's what you're implying. She just . . . forgot about me for a little while, that's all."

I thought about my mother back home. I wondered where she was, if she was roaming the house in the dark, calling my father's name.

"They sent her upstate. To a place called—"

"Harbrook Hill. Until 1964."

"That's right. She spent five years inside a stone cell with bars on the window and door. The one small saving grace was that the walls were solid and the bars on the window were tight, so only the little things could get in. And they did. For five whole years they crawled into her cell and fed on her."

I remembered the pockmarked flesh below Mom's collar. Not acne scars, after all, but spider bites. A shiver walked up my backside, and I fought the impulse to slap at it, to make sure it was *just* a shiver. "The doctors didn't do anything?"

Tiffany shrugged. "They checked her sheets for bed bugs and other infestations, but it all came up clean, of course, so they chalked the bumps off as some strange skin condition. Stress related. Psychosomatic. She learned to be quiet about her little friends, to pretend they weren't there, and by the time she was let out, she'd gotten very good at keeping still."

Mom was keeping plenty still now, except for the occasional thick bubble that popped beneath her nostrils. Her mouth was crusted with dried blood.

"Half a century she sat out on her corner," Tiffany said. "In the rain, in the snow, in the dead of summers where even the shade burned. Half a century, watching people like you go by. Her sweet children, she called you, like you were family, like the city was her house and everyone in it was right there with her, arm in arm. Half a century, waiting for whatever clock was ticking inside her to finally stop, so her half a life could end. She couldn't take it herself. No. Down deep, she was still that good little Catholic girl, and good little Catholic girls don't slit their wrists or they go to Hell. Makes no difference if they're already there. So don't pretend you know about suffering, Doctor. You don't. And don't tell me you don't deserve it. You knocked her house over, you came along and kicked it down, and I'm not sorry for what I did. I only wish I could make it *slower.*" Tiffany leaned forward. The back legs of her chair came an inch off the floorboards. Her front teeth showed in a white slice sharp enough to cut. "You're going to die, Doctor. You're going to die alone and far, far away, and your family will never even know why you didn't come home."

A switch clicked off in me. I went dark inside. I went dark like the locked house where I'd left my mother, and the next I knew I was off the couch with my hands around Tiffany's throat. Her chair slapped back to the ground. Her eyes widened as I squeezed. So did her mouth. I saw inside it to the black fang behind her molars. The fang was not hiding today. The fang was enjoying life in the sun. Feel that breeze come off the ocean, oh yeah, let it run right over you. Except there was no breeze in Tiffany's mouth. Tiffany was not breathing. I looked back up to her eyes. They had rolled to their whites. I let go. Tottered. Sat down on the couch.

Tiffany's head hung back on her neck. There were bruises on her throat and burst blood vessels on her cheeks. They looked like flowers, like red roses about to bloom. At least they weren't white. White roses were death roses and didn't belong on Earth. They belonged on black hillsides under endless, cruel starlight.

Tiffany coughed.

Her head rolled forward, her eyes rolled down, and her windpipe whistled harshly as she said, "Do you think I haven't tried that already? Do I look like a good little Catholic girl to you?"

PART FOUR
MY HUNGRY
FRIEND

46

I said nothing for a long time. The chalkboard of my brain had been swept completely bare. Beside me Mom twitched under her blankets. Her lips puffed out but remained sealed. Her mouth had been caked shut.

"Would you wipe that blood off so she can breathe?" Tiffany said softly. "Please?"

I went into the kitchen. There was a washcloth on the oven door and seeing it there, hanging in the same place that washcloths were hung in my house, gave me a dizzy spell that laid me up against the counter. Heavy red clouds clotted the window. They looked lower. Closer. *My hungry friend follows me where I go*, I thought, *and where I am I do not know.*

I found a salad bowl inside one of the cupboards. I rinsed the bowl out because there was a dead spider in it, then I filled the bowl with warm water and carried it into the living room along with the washcloth.

"Be gentle," Tiffany said as I wiped her mother's mouth. "Her teeth—her new teeth—they're still coming in. They've been coming in a long time. I don't think they'll ever stop."

I finished dabbing away the blood.

"Thank you," said Tiffany.

I put the washcloth in the bowl and dried my hands off on my jeans. "What are you?" I asked.

"I am my mother's child." There was something in Tiffany's voice that had not been there before, something beneath the slight, coarse whistle of her breath that might have been fear. "And I am my father's child, too."

"Who is he?"

"*He* is not a he, and He is not of Earth. He swims the skies of His world on wings of silk and shadow. You know the world I speak of. You've seen it. Soon it will be your world as well."

47

Tiffany was not used to telling her story—I recognized that straightaway. She had the look my mom used to get after misplacing something in the early days of her Alzheimer's. A confused, *searching* look. With Tiffany, it wasn't an item she was trying to find but a place to start. She began finally with a word she always seemed to return to, a word she used to divide herself from everyone else.

"People," she said. "People think you get what you deserve. Sure, they'll *say* otherwise. They'll act like they believe in bad luck, but they don't deep down. Not really. For them the great cosmic wheel of chance only spins if you set it into motion, and if it gives you a bad roll, well, it's your own damn fault for playing the game in the first place. You get mugged and that's *so* awful, you must have been *so* scared, but what part of town you were in? And why were you out so late? You get cancer, and the condolences roll in, but inside their heads people are counting how many cigarettes you smoked or cheeseburgers you put away. Never mind if it's pancreatic cancer or a brain tumor. You must have done *something* to invite it. I heard a woman say once that the Jews signed up for the Holocaust before they were born. Like they got together with Hitler as their souls were being packaged up for shipping, and said, 'Sure, buddy, stoke those ovens, get them nice and hot.'

"People want to believe there's a reason for the shitty things that happen. They'll tell themselves whatever they have to so they can go on pretending the universe isn't just a big man with a big cock waiting to bend you over, whip you raw with a starbelt, and have his way with you. But sometimes you just get fucked. Sometimes cancer invites itself, and you wake up one day to find it snuggled inside you. That's how my mom got me. She didn't sing the Lord's Prayer backwards, she didn't dance naked in a graveyard at midnight, and she didn't read from a flesh-bound book excavated from some forgotten underground city. She was an old widow one day, and an old inseminated widow the next. Something had blown her way and planted itself inside her, like a black seed in the crack of a sidewalk."

I stayed quiet. Tiffany had found her course, and I did not want to steer her from it.

"I was ten years old when I got my funny tooth. That's what I called it. My funny tooth. Before it came in I didn't know I was any different than my brothers and sisters. There were nine of us, all with our own last names, jam packed into a rickety house in Worcester. I liked to wiggle my funny tooth with my tongue, and what was really funny about the tooth, more than anything, was that sometimes it wiggled all by itself. I told my foster dad about it, but he didn't listen. He didn't care about what I had in my mouth unless he put it there, and he put it there almost every night. I was his favorite. His little Abby. Until the tooth got bigger and gave his prick a nice *nick*. He got funny himself after that. He stopped using the bathroom downstairs and if he wanted something from the walk-in pantry, he always made one of us fetch it for him. He itched at himself constantly. Especially his crotch. He started carrying around a rolled-up newspaper and slapping at the walls, the table, the air. Once he even went at his wife with it. He chased her clear out of the house and refused to let her back in until she was 'clean.'

"I slept peacefully for two nights. On the third night he came in the dark and stood in the doorway calling my name, like he wasn't sure if I was there. Like he couldn't see into the room at all. 'Abby, what did you do to me? Abby, it hurts. Abby, I'm scared. What did you *do*, Abby?' I didn't say anything back, and neither did my sisters. We were all awake and hoping he'd go and leave us be, but he stepped inside instead. He came in *real* slow, all tiptoes, and when he let go of the frame, when the last part of him passed across the threshold, he wasn't there anymore. His shadow was gone. The nightlight touched the hall again. One of my sisters got up and looked for him, but she didn't look very hard—not that it would have made a difference. He wasn't hiding in the closet, and he sure hadn't put on an invisibility cloak. He'd simply vanished. A week went by without his face at the table, and then our foster mom sat all us boys and girls down and told us, irritably, that her no good husband had run off and she couldn't possibly raise nine kids alone on her teeny-tiny government paycheck."

Tiffany paused, looking past me, even though past me there was only a bare wall.

"The dreams came after I started bleeding. I was living with a couple and their two kids in Milton. Well-to-do family. Nice enough. The dad a bit distracted and the mom a bit bored. I think they would have adopted me for real—it was on their to-do list, somewhere between take Joseph to karate and get Sarah braces. But then He found me, or maybe He had been there all along, just waiting for me to get ripe." The burst-blood vessels on Tiffany's cheeks had softened to pink. Her throat was a smooth creamy white, without a trace of fingerprints. "It began as sleepwalking. I'd go to bed and wake up in my closet or the bathtub, or I'd come out for breakfast in the morning and Joey would tell everyone how I stood over his bed like a creep in the night. We'd all laugh, me included. Oh, that wacky Abigail, what shenanigans will she get up to next? Cue the laugh track. But then my sleep activities became more . . . active. I'd run laps up and down the hall. I'd bang my head on windows hard enough to crack the glass—but never hard enough to leave a mark on myself or wake myself up. I could not be woken. One time I took off my clothes and crawled naked into bed with Mom and Dad—they had me call them Mom and Dad and got sad looking if I ever used their first names, like I'd let them down. Well, they took me to a therapist, and a lot of the stuff I said or didn't say convinced the therapist that I'd had 'not such a good time' in my last home. My 'not such a good time' became the explanation for all of my nightly disturbances, which would supposedly go away once I learned to feel 'safe and loved.' In the meantime to prevent me from hurting myself, it was decided that a lock on my door was for the best. With my wanderings confined to my room, sleeping-me got cranky. I would flick the lights on and off, tear up the carpet, scratch at the walls. But all this was just foreplay, the first playful touches of whatever was taking me at night. I remembered nothing between the time I closed my eyes and opened them in the morning, except for the feeling that I had been somewhere else, *something* else.

"The first dream happened on January, 14ᵗʰ, 1970. My thirteenth birthday. The house had settled down early, but I lay awake in bed. It is very clear even now. My funny tooth—my secret—tingled strangely in my mouth. It felt like an entire limb had fallen asleep under my gums. Pins and needles, but not unpleasant. Soothing. Purring. I got up. I walked to the window. It seemed very important that I look outside. My body was a bladder, full, heavy, and the only way to relieve it was to look outside. But when I pulled back the curtain, outside was not there. Not *my* outside. The backyard, the leafy oak, the tire swing, all these things were gone. In their place was a field of tall grass with blades so thin and pale they were almost see through, like your hand when you cup your palm over a flashlight. The sky glowed in them. The sky filled them up. They were pouring over like cups of liquid fire. I was pouring over, too. Spilling out through my bedroom window. I spread my arms and my arms spread themselves thin on the air, bearing me up, melting me into the warm night. I rose higher, floating on the wind as oil floats on water, until the sky began to tear above me, giving way to bluish black emptiness, to stars. There I swam, in the crack between the cold of space and the warmth of the world below. My shadow spanned entire vistas. All that it touched, I saw. From saw-toothed mountain ranges that had never felt snow or sunlight to oceans as dark and still as stained glass . . . and down into those oceans, to ancient unbelievable beings that glided quietly on planes of silence. I was nightfall, true nightfall, for a world that did not turn, a world that fed on its own heat and light and wandered alone among the stars.

"I woke not in my house but on a beach miles away, at dawn. I had walked across town in my sleep, or something in my sleep had walked *me,* only to flee as the sun tipped the Atlantic. The first person I came across—a jogger—let me borrow her phone. I called my foster parents, who took me home and installed heavy locks on my window so I couldn't crawl out of it again. They had no better solutions and they certainly couldn't explain how I had gotten from my room on the second floor to the ground without anything to climb down. It was as if I had flown. The next night I had the dream again—I swam the red skies of that other world—and I woke to find myself west in Dedham, in the garden by Wigham Pond. There was crusted blood on my knuckles, but no cuts anywhere on my body. Later I discovered that I had shattered my window. My foster parents, woken by the noise, had rushed to my bedroom to find me already gone. I told them I was sorry. They told me it was okay. Then they boarded my window and took away my chair, which they believed I had used to smash out the glass. I knew better, though. I had used my fists.

"Night rolled around. I escaped again and came to at sunrise in the back of a police car. The nails on my hands were wiggly as baby teeth, and blood had dried under them. I'd dug my fingers between the boards and walls and pried my way free—all from the inside. The police officer had found me halfway to Boston, shuffling along without bending my elbows or knees. When he picked me up by the armpits, my legs kept moving stiffly in the air. I scratched his face and left deep furrows. I did not speak a word to him until daylight cracked open the night sky, and by then he had found out who I was and where I belonged.

"My foster parents got permission to sedate me. It didn't help. I pulled off the doorknob and used it to smash holes in the door, which was deadbolted. They took me to a sleep clinic, where doctors stuck stuff on my head and strapped me to a cot. I slept soundly through the night. They took me home, and I was right back at the door as soon as the sun went down, only this time I used my skull. I could no longer get out the window because that had been boarded with heavy plywood slabs, each one three-inches thick and riddled with nails. Finally, Mom and Dad threw in the towel. They had their kids, their real kids, to think about. I had a new home by March, and by November, the dreams started again. Dreams of that other world, where I swam beneath stars on wings as wide as the horizon, wings that made no sound, no wind, as they rolled against reddened skies. This family was less understanding of my escape artistry and my potential for violence while unconscious. After sleeping-me dug a fingernail into my foster dad's eye, they put me back in the box, return to sender. For the next few years it went like that. A new place, a few months of calm if not peace as I waited for the dreams to return, for my nightself to grow restless and walk the dark Earth. I tired of it. It is a terrible thing to lay down to sleep and not know where you will wake up. Don't you agree, Doctor?"

I agreed.

"I tried to kill myself for the first time when I was sixteen. I drew a warm bath, cut my forearms from the wrist to the elbow, and instead of the rest I had hoped for, I dreamed of Him, of *It*, that vast and shapeless thing that eclipses the stars and gives night to a sunless world. I woke in a cold bath, the water filmed over with my blood. Only a faint line showed on each forearm where I'd used the razor. I tried again two weeks later in the woods. I took a bus to White Mountain. It was a warm day in August. I hung myself from a thick tree branch with a length of rope, and for an aeon I floated on red skies like a malignant leaf on a pond. Then I sat up on the forest floor, sucking in breath, the noose still around my neck. Its other end remained tied to the branch, which had cracked and fallen from my weight. The ground was an icy gruel of mud and leaves, and my summer clothes had frozen to my skin. Every inch of me had gone purple, rigid. It was slow going trudging back to civilization. By the time I made it, I looked myself again except for the rags on my body. It was November. I had been hanging in the woods, by my throat, for three long months. Swaying there as the seasons changed around me. I didn't even have rope burns to show for it. What I did have was understanding. My dreams were not dreams, and my nightself was not myself at all. When I slept, I saw through something else's eyes. And that something else . . . it saw through mine. I was its window to Earth, and it liked the view. It would not let me draw the curtains."

Tiffany regarded me. "You've been awfully quiet, Doctor. You're not dozing off on me, are you?"

"No." If anything, I was dozing off on myself and my current situation. Her story was sad and frightening, and it told me a lot, though not what I had come here to learn. The mother always still. The daughter always moving. Neither of them with a place to call home.

"Well," Tiffany said. "My family was not pleased to see me back after so long. The court decided to send me to a group home, as good a place as any for a runaway like me. It was there I met Lisa. She was a troubled girl, like me, though I suppose there's no one on this planet who is *quite* like me. We became friends. We had no one else. She was always in the cups, Lisa. Do you know that expression? *In the cups*? Or are you too young?" Tiffany paused for a moment. "Anyway, I didn't like to drink because alcohol put me to sleep and I did not trust sleep, even then, when I was new to the group home and the dreams were leaving me alone. But I liked blow. Blow kept me zip-zapping all night long, kept me myself during those dark hours when the window opened to that *other* world and that thing, that great and awful thing, walked inside me. Lisa, she had a few connections in town, and one evening we got very high and decided our lips were too nice not to share. We kissed. Deeply. Too deeply. The next day Lisa's tongue was swollen and she couldn't talk well. She could scream fine, though. She saw something in her room, hanging from the ceiling, that made her scream right out of the group home and into a straitjacket. The straitjacket soon disappeared, Lisa with it. The newspapers had a tizzy. They called her Lady Houdini, but Lisa had escaped more than the hospital. She was the second person I sent away."

I saw myself bound in a straitjacket, lying on my back and howling under a bloody panorama of sky. I swallowed. "How many others have you sent away?"

"Only one," she said, a slight tilt to her head. "But you're still hanging on. Aren't you getting tired yet? Wouldn't it be so much easier to just let go?"

"What is it?" I said. "That thing in your mouth. What does it do?"

"Do you really think I know the answer to that?"

"I think you have a pretty good idea, seeing as you've had half a century years to think about it."

Tiffany's hands opened and closed at the ends of her duct-taped arms. "My tooth is the part of me that belongs to my father, and what belongs to my father does not belong to Earth. He is not allowed here, don't you see? That's why He made Himself a daughter, so He could walk where He is forbidden to walk. His world orbits no star. He is night there, and like the night, He is driven out by the sun."

"That doesn't answer my question."

"But it does. My tooth cannot be on Earth. Yet it is on Earth. To be cut by it, to be *opened* by it, is to unlock a door that was never meant to exist. You're standing in that door now, Doctor, and when you step to the other side, when the last piece of you lets go of this world and you cross over, the door will shut behind you for good. That is the only way the door will shut, and there is no way back."

But there was. I had been there, to that lunatic place beyond our stars. I'd felt its spoiled growth beneath my feet, and I'd tasted the depth of its hunger in a pair of yellow searchlight eyes. And I'd found my way back. My mother had guided me home. I clutched the house key hanging from my throat, bundling it up in my shirts. "Marianne, your mom, she's still here. No door ever shut behind her."

"No door ever opened for her, either. Only a few small cracks. She got just enough of my father from me to keep her around—and to grow a new set of teeth. For her Earth remains Earth . . . but with a few extra visitors." Tiffany's posture deflated. Something pent up had run out of her in the telling of her story. She stared at the woman on the couch and for a moment seemed to forget how to speak. When she did, her voice was so quiet I could barely hear her. "We've only had a year, me and my mom. I didn't know she was there. I'd looked for her long ago, found all there was to know about her, my birth, everything but where she went after Harbrook Hill. I thought she was gone. I'd been moving around, I'd never stopped moving since I was a kid. Then I came back to Boston. I came back and one day as I was taking a walk through the city, I heard a voice. '*My sweet child,*' it said, '*my Abigail.*' I hadn't been Abigail for decades, and she hadn't seen me since she could hold me in one arm, but she knew me. She recognized me all the same."

I understood then, at last. There was no help to be found or forced. If Tiffany knew of a way to shut out that other world, she would have done so for her mother. She would not have let her only loved one wither on the street. There it was. As simple as that. I did not need to plead or pull out my knife. The truth was lying right beside me, scarred by spider bites. All that I had managed to accomplish by coming here was to share my pain and fear with those who had hurt me and made me afraid. I looked down at the old woman bundled next to my leg.

I kept looking.

"What?" said Tiffany.

Mom's nose was no longer bleeding. Her wayward, rolling eye had come to a rest beneath its half-shut lid.

"*What?*"

I reached out with one hand, one slow and slightly trembling hand, and lifted Mom's head. There was blood on the fabric where it had rested. Beneath her hair—in the back—her scalp was soft. Uneven. I remembered my first kick, the crack of bone as Mom's skull hit the wall. She was dead. After all those years sitting on her corner, hiding from that other world, Mom was dead. Not from one of His children but from a boot heel. I got up on legs that had forgotten how to hold me. I pulled the knife out of my jacket and walked to Tiffany, who was sitting completely still, completely quiet. She remained that way as I cut the duct tape from her arms, then she walked past me, sat down on the floor by the couch, laid her head on her mother's chest, and did not move again.

I stood there for a minute, watching her.

I turned to leave.

She said, "There's one thing I forgot to mention, Doctor. One tiny thing. My friend Lisa, from the group home, she had a boyfriend. The morning after she nicked her tongue on my funny tooth, the two of them were together. Everyone thought he ran off with her when she disappeared from the hospital. Because he disappeared, too. A few days after her vanishing act, he dropped off the face of the Earth, too."

Tiffany twisted around to look at me, and fulfilled her promise. She showed me her smile. It cracked her face open and collected the tears running down her cheeks.

"The door is inside you, Doctor. The door is inside you, and it is wide open. You haven't been intimate with anyone, have you? You haven't slipped your little key into somebody's lock . . . have you?"

48

Tiffany's last words were a cold wind in my heart and at my back. I left her apartment in a run. Not once did it cross my mind to call a cab even though Cassie lived across the river in Somerville. My head was full with every moment I had shared with her since our one night together. Her distractedness on Thursday evening, her jitteriness to leave the house (what if she had been *more* than simply stir crazy? What if she had seen something that had gotten deep under her skin) . . . then her zombie shuffle the following morning, as if she hadn't slept a minute all night. And, finally, our last encounter. I had come home early prepared to tell her I was sick, only to discover that *she* was sick. A fever, she'd told me, and at the door I'd kissed her to shut her up. To make her leave. *I just thought it would have been nice to go somewhere*, she'd said, her voice sad, regretful. *Would have been nice, would have been*, and had her lips been hot? Or had she been lying about the fever and coming down with something else, something much worse?

The clouds had swallowed their fill and were beginning to burst. Stars winked through the rips and tears in their bellies, shining down from constellations far cruder, sharper, than the constellations of our universe. I ran through the gutted night, the streets around me bathed in red. My feet ached inside my father's boots. My brow dripped beneath my father's hat, and at some point the hat came off and flew away, never to be seen again. I did not notice its departure, did not have a chance to say goodbye. The holes that Mr. Buckteeth had put in my body stung as my sweat got into them. I could no longer see my breath in front of my face. Boston's temperature was on the rise. The bitterness of March was melting along with the dark, giving way to humid, sluggish heat as the light of that other world soaked into the city.

Then I reached the river, and the light went out.

All of it.

49

I was on the bridge to Harvard Square, Boston at my back, Cambridge in my future, and the Charles flowing like a giant open artery beneath me, when the shadow fell. Or perhaps *rose* would be more accurate. It came not from the east as night comes but from the west, moving against the rotation of the world. The horizon went first, as if someone took a pencil and marked a line where the landscape ends and the sky begins. Then the line spilled upwards, spreading with such great slowness that my eyes could not spot the growth. I had to blink in order to digest the change, take it in one bite at a time. If I tried to swallow any more than that at once, my brain choked. I continued to jog, some part of me still intent on reaching Cassie's, but not for long. As the clouds in the distance were blotted out and the land beneath them plunged from view, I stopped and clutched onto the parapet and watched the edge of the planet rush closer, dragged by the black silhouette rising over Boston. It stretched so wide it seemed to curve with the Earth. It spanned farther than I could see, than I could dream.

But most unbelievable of all was the way it moved. Waves ran through the shadow, powerful, sinuous, rolling north and south with terrible symmetry. To call the waves enormous would be to call Pluto cold. The waves were Everests on an ocean of darkness, and the darkness had a head, a smooth fat sickle, a half moon in which two volcanic eyes burned . . . eyes as red as the boiling ether beyond the clouds . . . all-seeing eyes that stared down from the heavens like the eyes of God.

He swims the skies of His world on wings of silk and shadow.

I backed away from the parapet, off the sidewalk, and into the road. If there had been traffic, that would have been the end of me, but the bridge was deserted at this thin hour on Saturday morning, which was falling out of the light just when it should have been saying hello to dawn. He blacked out the stars. He cloaked all that passed beneath Him. As His shadow swept forward, His eyes lit the river and the land on either side. The water steamed under His baleful red gaze. I tripped on the curb and continued to crawl back until I stopped against the eastern parapet. The bridge fell into darkness and then flashed a hot bright scarlet, and for one shuddering moment, time and space ceased to exist. He looked down upon me through the clouds, that final thinning barrier between our worlds, and His eyes met mine. I drowned in them, melted in them. I spun around and around in them, unraveling in a whirlpool of blood and flame. When they finally spit me out, there were no stars left in the sky. The only light anywhere was the light cast by the city.

Night had been delivered to Boston on black wings, and to the east, where the Charles dumped into the Atlantic, no sun rose to challenge it.

No.

Him.

No sun rose to challenge *Him*.

50

How I went on after that, I do not know. My body crawled with unseen spiders. I felt them on my skin and under my skin, in my bones and in the pathways of my veins. They itched deep in my marrow, remnants of the unfathomable consciousness that had reached down and touched me from the sky. When I opened my mouth to release the scream locked inside, I expected a scuttling flood to come with it and cover my face, my eyes. But no flood came, and no scream either, just a gasp and some spittle. Then I got up. I gathered the rags of my sanity, and I got up. For Cassie.

The dark was thick as mist, and warmer than any dark I have ever known. It swaddled me like the blankets Mom had worn. I made my way by street lamps and headlights and the occasional glow of a window. There were far fewer lit windows than there should have been, for Cambridge was far less than it appeared on the surface. Its walls housed the same unearthly night that lay over the city. Behind every brick, under every cobblestone waited that other world, so close that I could almost hear the architecture straining to hold it. I did not run out of fear that the sidewalk would crack beneath me like an eggshell. I did not look up either, afraid I would see the movement that I sensed everywhere overhead, the smooth, black movement of the timeless being that brought night as He rode between the stratosphere and stars. Knowing He was there beyond the clouds was enough.

Living under His shadow, save me, was enough.

51

Cassie rented an apartment on Craigie Street, and her building was the only one on the entire block that had lights on behind its windows. Seeing those lights surrounded in so much darkness was like coming to a lighthouse after being lost at sea, but underneath my relief, my worry burned all the brighter. She was awake, and what kind of unspeakable things could keep sleep at bay at five o'clock on a weekend morning?

I nearly fell as I ran up the crooked steps to her porch. I pounded on the door, supercharged by the fear running through me. She had gone down into her basement—did she have a basement?—and made a bucktoothed friend. She had reached into her closet for her robe, and something had yanked her out of her bedroom, her apartment, the world. She was walking in utter night under that old insane God whose eyes never closed, whose jealous gaze was turned forever toward Earth from His terrible throne on the rim of the universe. She was lost and dying and afraid—she was all of these things at once in a thousand different scenarios, because of *me*, and then she was at the door.

"Mike?" she said. The glow of her television haloed her in a ghostly blue, so that she seemed hardly there. "Jesus, Mike, the sun's barely even up. What are you—"

She got stuck, and I don't blame her. My appearance must have been a lot to swallow, from my disheveled hair and shaved face to the holes in my jeans and leather jacket. And my cowboy boots, couldn't forget those. Meanwhile, I was trying to understand how the sun could be up for her and not for me and how her breath could show on the air when my entire body was smothered in warm sweat. And simpler things . . . like the color that had been leeched from her dark cheeks and the used tissue balled up in her left hand.

"The flu," I said. "You've got the flu."

That unstuck her. "Yeah, and it fucking sucks. Now come in. It's freezing."

The door was inside me, and only me. It had not opened in her. Not yet.

"No," I said.

"What do you mean, 'no?' Come in. Let's talk."

"I didn't come here to talk. I came here to tell you."

"Tell me what?" Her face wore a complex mix of emotions and fever. Confusion wrestled with frustration along her brow. Her mouth didn't know how to set itself. "Tell me what, Mike?"

"It's not going to work."

"What are you talking about? You're scaring me." She reached out. I took a step back down her stoop.

"Don't. Just don't. Listen, it would have been nice, it was a nice idea, but it's done now. There's nothing left."

She came out onto the welcome mat in her bare feet. Goosebumps made Braille in the open crevasse of her nightgown, and even now—more than ever—I wanted to run my fingers there. To share my fevered night with her fevered body. "What happened, Mike? What's going on? Is it . . . oh God, is it your mother?"

"My mother has nothing to do with it. I'm telling you it's done. We're done."

She shook her head. There were tears in her eyes. "You're not making any sense. You're not—look at you—you're not yourself."

I saw my boots smash into Mom's upturned face. I could feel the crunch like it was stuck to my heel, like it was a wad of gum I couldn't wipe off . . . and maybe I wasn't myself, but the world wasn't itself either so what difference did it make? I took another step back. Cassie came a step forward. "I don't care about you," I said. "I never did. I was just lonely, and you were there. You could have been anyone."

She stopped. Mercifully. "You're lying. I don't believe you."

"I don't really care what you believe. I got what I wanted so you can go away. Just go away."

"Fuck you," she said. "You don't get to show up out of nowhere and tell me to go away. No. That's not how it works. You want to be done, fine, that's fine, but you're the one who gets to walk. So fucking walk, Mike. Get the fuck out of here."

I did.

I backed down to the street, turned, and walked away in the dark that was mine and mine alone. I listened for the slam of her door, but I never heard it, and soon I was running again. Running and clutching onto the key around my throat and realizing, as its teeth bit into my hand, that Cassie had been wearing hers, too.

Cassie had been wearing her key, too.

52

I was sprinting with nowhere in mind when headlights splashed on me and I crashed onto the hood of a car. A third light, smaller, shined on the car's roof. A taxi. The driver rolled down his window to yell, and I tossed what was left of the money Tiffany had paid me into his lap, including the fifty dollar bill I'd tried to give to Mom.

"Take me home," I said.

I don't remember much of the drive back except that it started off dark and grew darker as the street lamps shut down and the other cars turned off their headlights. Boston was waking up for the day, but the day had never arrived. Not for me. The time for sunrise had come and gone, leaving my world behind. I closed my eyes. All I wanted was to sleep.

Sleep and forget.

The cab dropped me off in front of my house. I unlocked the door, then I sat down in the doorway. It smelled bad inside. Like an egg cracked open and rotten. It smelled so bad my head swam. I couldn't get in a breath. There was something hissing in the kitchen, soft and low, hissing in the kitchen with Dinah . . . fee fi fiddly I oh . . . the gas, oh God, the gas.

I stood up, holding my shirt over my nose against that rotten egg smell, and they put that smell in so you know, they put that smell in so you know-oh-oh-oh. The furniture got in my way as I crossed the living room. Everything was wobbly, drunk, and me most of all. I shoved and stumbled through, bouncing off the couch and bookcase before I reached the kitchen. There was an open carton of eggs—actual eggs—on the counter and a cool pan on the stove. All four burners had been turned on high but left unlit. For how long? How *long*? I switched them off and then gravity took me on a funny do-si-do, turning me to the window that I'd shut that morning in order to seal the crack. Just like I'd sealed the cracks in the walls and around the basement door, leaving the gas nowhere to go as it gobbled the oxygen in the house. Nowhere but—"

No no no no.

I pushed off the counter like a swimmer kicking off in a pool, and I glided through the living room in a dreamy fog of terror, that song going around my head on a clipped, lunatic loop. Someone in the kitchen. Someone I know. Someone in the kitchen with Dinah, strumming on the old banjo. I fell on the stairs. Got up. Fell again. I had no voice to call out with, no air to breathe. An enormous foot stood on my chest, crushing my heart between my ribs like garlic in a garlic press. I crawled to the office and pulled myself up by the doorknob. It was six in the morning, and six in the morning was clicking time for the keys on my mother's typewriter.

They were not clicking now.

They were quiet.

She sat at her desk with her head tilted back and her eyes rolled up to the ceiling. She looked like Tiffany had looked strangled in her chair. I dragged her across the room and opened the window and stuck her mouth against the screen so she could take the air while it was fresh.

She didn't want it.

53

The paramedics came. And the police. And the coroner. They asked a lot of questions I don't remember. I must have answered well enough because they let me stay behind when they took my mother. Neighbors stood on their porches in the dark and watched the parade drive off into the night, which, for them, was morning. Spiders crawled on rooftops, and things slithered low and half seen in the shadows. I had an idea that if I threw a rock, I could knock over one of those Victorians like a bowling pin. It all felt very thin, and it made my head hurt to think about, so I stopped. I went upstairs to my bedroom, but my bedroom wasn't there. Beyond the threshold waited the same night that sat outside the house, only darker, much darker. Past the front door, a few bright lights remained strewn over the city. Past *this* door, there was no city and so there was nothing left to shine but the stars that had been cloaked by Tiffany's father. My room was no longer a part of Earth. It had been zipped up in a black bag and taken away.

I didn't care.

I was tired.

I went back down the hall to my mother's room, crawled into bed, and fell asleep in her smell to dreams where I was lost with no hand to guide me home.

54

That was the last time I slept under actual covers, and it feels like a long time ago. I woke hungry and went downstairs to cook the eggs that had been left out on the counter. I scrambled them on a pan over the stove, then I took a seat at the table beside a bowl of half-eaten oatmeal. I stared at the bowl for an empty moment before taking out my phone. It no longer worked. Where the date and hour should have been, the screen showed a small searching icon. Nor was there a single bar of reception. It was as if I were flying on a plane instead of sitting in the kitchen of my house. The microwave had also boarded the plane. Its clock blinked zeros.

I ate my breakfast in the dark, and after a while I found myself watching a dawn of sorts.

A gash opened to the west, and warm red light spilled through the wound. The clouds had cleared, just like Cassie promised they would over the weekend, leaving the stars full purchase of the sky. They glimmered hard and bright in their bloody void. There was a cruel, forsaken beauty to them, and to the landscape they overlooked. Soaring, sailboat leaves rocked in the distance. White fields wandered off into a translucent haze, interrupted in places by great bone trees standing with outstretched arms. Here and there were the silhouettes of buildings, but silhouettes is all they were. The dawn—if such an event could be called dawn, without a sun—blew them apart like smoke in a strong wind. Boston had been scrubbed out of existence. Only a scattered afterimage remained, and not even that for long. As the night fled on silent black wings, dragging a forked tail across the sky, it left a new world in its wake.

Savin Hill was gone.

The backyard was gone.

My house stood alone in a wasteland of white flowers and yawning ravines.

55

I ate my eggs.

I sat at the kitchen table, sipping coffee from an I♥Boston mug, and I ate my eggs in full view of that other world outside the window. The eggs tasted good. When they were gone, I washed my plate and stuck it in the dish rack to dry. I did the same with the pan, the mug, and the leftover bowl of oatmeal, then I went upstairs to tidy my mother's room. The outfit I'd worn last night was piled on the floor. I put the jeans and shirt in the laundry basket and set the boots on the shoe rack. With so much out of place, it felt right to put a few things in order, and I suppose that's what I was doing. Putting things in order while they were still there. While I was still there.

I got a fresh change of clothes from the drier (the clothes in my room were well out of reach) and had a shower. A long one. My last one. When I was done, I folded the towel neatly over the rail and stepped out into the hall. From there I went to the office. Everything was how I'd left it. I closed the window, drew the blackout curtains against the starry red sky, and righted the fallen chair. My next stop was outside. I was ready to leave. To let go and let the door shut behind me, like Tiffany said. As I pushed the chair back into the desk, my eyes stopped on my mother's old IBM typewriter and something whispered to me with a voice that I felt but did not hear, a voice like a warm, fleeting touch. I lowered myself slowly into the seat. The last page she'd written sat in the carriage. Not a poem, and not prose either, just one sentence repeated over and over again, filling the space between the margins.

I found you. I found you. I found you. I found you. I found
you. I found you. I found you. I found you. I found you. I
found you. I found you. I found you. I found you. I found
you. I found you. I found you. I found you. I found you. I
found you. I found you. I found you. I found you. I found
you. I found you. I found you. I found you. I found you. I
found you. I found you. I found you. I found you. I found
you. I found you. I found you. I found you. I found you. I
found you. I found you. I found you. I found you. I found
you. I found you. I found you. I found you. I found you. I
found you. I found you. I found you. I found you. I found
you. I found you. I found you. I found you. I found you. I
foundyou. I found you. I found you. I found you. I found
you. I found you. I found you. I found you. Ifound you. I
found you. I found you.I found you. I found you. I found
you. I foundyou. I found you. Ifound you. I fo und you.I
found you. I found you. I foundyouI foundyou.I found.you.
Ifound you.I found you I foundyou.I foundyou. I foundyouI
foundyou.I foundyou. Ifound you.I found you I foundyou..I
found you.I foundyouI foun dyou.I foundyou. Ifound you.I
foundyou I foundyou.I foujnd youI f.oundyouI foundyou.I
fuiondyopu. Ifoudn you.Ifoundyou U foundyou.Ifound youI
fuonfyou.IyoufoundIfn ou md You. ifoundyuo.IfounduoyouI

I took the page out of the typewriter. I held it for a long
time. Then I put it to the side, selected a fresh sheet from the
ream in her drawer, and loaded the sheet into the carriage, as
she always used to when done writing for the day. This was
part of her ritual, perhaps the most vital part, for it was a

promise. That there would be a new poem. Another story. A tomorrow.

As I touched the keys, I could almost feel her hand on my shoulder.

There you are.

Come on now.

I started to type.

56

I put down twenty pages before I took a break to empty my bladder. After another fifteen, I was hungry and thirsty. I went downstairs to grab what I could from the kitchen and bring it back to the office. Bottles of sparkling water, loaves of bread, peanut butter, jerky. I filled two paper shopping bags until they were so heavy I had to carry them underarm instead of by the handle. My phone lay on the table where I'd set it during breakfast. I picked it up out of simple habit and hit the button that lit the screen. The clock was still out of sorts, and the reception was in no better shape, but something had come through to me, somehow. A voice mail, time-stamped 5:03 Saturday evening.

From Lucy.

"Hi Mike," she said. "I hope I'm not bothering you, but I was at the office this afternoon, getting stuff organized for next week in case you're ready to come back—it's okay if you aren't, I know you're taking some time, and I'm glad you are.

Really. Anyway, I was at the office, and the phone rang. It was Tony. Shawna's dad. I didn't recognize him at first . . . his voice was so little, and he's so *big*, you know. He wanted to talk to you, but I said you were out on account of family stuff, and he said that's what he wanted to talk to you about. Family stuff. He said he went like you asked, he took her like you asked and you were right, but they caught it on time. He said that over and over, they caught it on time, and then he told me to thank you. It was pretty mystifying. All I can figure is Shawna must be sick, but she's going to be all right, and that's good news. Well. Take care of yourself, Mike."

I stood there a while after the message ended.

Yes. Yes, it was good news.

I put the phone back down, carried my bags upstairs, and took a seat at the typewriter. While I ate, I wrote Lucy a recommendation letter. It wasn't much, but it was all I had left to give. The letter rests on the desk where it will be found should I never be seen again.

57

How Lu's message reached me without any signal I cannot say, but I have an idea my phone worked fine as long as I wasn't near it. The clock on the microwave was a different story. Knock that sucker out, and he's down for the count until you put the time back in manually. Smartphones on the other hand are built to be on constant lookout, their brainwaves blipping from cell towers to satellites. They'll keep ticking unless they're a mile over Earth or something is throwing them off, and I thought there was a good chance my presence could be doing just that.

I didn't belong to Earth anymore, after all.

Sixty pages into my story (that is how I have come to measure time, by the thinning of the ream in the drawer and the thickening of the stack on the desk), I got up to have a sit down on the toilet. The smell I made was as mean as a schoolyard bully. I closed the bathroom behind me and as the latch clicked I felt . . . you know when you cough and a bit of phlegm comes loose in your chest? I felt something *slide*, both inside and outside of me, and I turned to find red light leaking through the cracks around the door. The light was also coming from my mother's bedroom, and in much greater quantity, for I'd left her door ajar. I hurried back to the typewriter.

Now the hallway is gone, too, as well as downstairs.

In the shrinking house that is my world, the office is my last and brightest room.

58

Forty pages ago, I paused to stretch and have a sandwich. My back ached and there were blisters on my fingertips from striking the keys. I crossed my legs on the floor and found myself looking at the closet, thinking of the poem I had crumpled and thrown away, the poem I had taken as proof of my mother's failing mind. Sonlight on the walls. *Son*light. Had she been writing about me? Had her jumbled spelling been her way of expressing some feeling she could no longer quite grasp? Yes, I believed so, and the falling of the sonlight, the darkening of the halls, the contrast of warmth and cold . . . I should never have left her alone. I thought of the open carton of eggs on the counter and the half-eaten bowl of oatmeal on the table. She'd come downstairs for breakfast, switched on the burners without lighting them, and at some point the typewriter had called her upstairs. This much I knew for certain. What I did not know was if the gas had been an accident or intentional. The night she wet herself, she'd spoken about Sylvia Plath, who had stuck her head in the oven, and Virginia Woolf, who had put rocks in her pockets (pockets in her rocks) and walked into the river. Both were writers she'd admired, and their deaths had clearly hovered somewhere in the haze of her consciousness. But that bowl of oatmeal. My mind kept returning to that bowl of oatmeal. I couldn't get her to swallow the stuff unless I spooned it into her mouth. If she'd planned on checking out, why make her most hated food her last meal? Why not have the eggs she always wanted, especially when she had already gotten eggs from the refrigerator? On the other hand, if she'd simply been moving about the kitchen on autopilot, taking things out, turning things on, how had she managed to stay on one track long enough to hunt down a bowl, mix oatmeal and water, manage the microwave, fetch a spoon, and finally sit down to eat? And then there was the matter of what she'd written. Three words, *I found you, I found you,* repeated like a crumbling prayer as she suffocated at her desk. Three words that might have been meant for me. A message? A suicide note? Or simply the confused side effect of breathing in too much gas at the kitchen table?

I didn't know.

I would never know.

There was another question, one that had nagged at me from the very beginning, and as I washed down the crusts of my sandwich, I realized I was still staring at the closet. The last time I'd opened it, I'd ended up someplace dark and wet that smelled of bad fish. I got up. The door filled out its frame. Moisture had bloated the wood years ago, and every crack had pinched tightly shut. I took the loose, flat-nosed handle with fingers that hurt to bend, fingers that felt thirty years older than the rest of my body. And I pulled.

The closet was an open window.

The window looked out on my new world. Rolling hills of gouged black rock. Deep ravines populated by shadows. A night sky wild with stars. Roses whitened the dark skin of the wasteland, and for the first time I saw where the wasteland ended. In the distance a mountain stood etched against the red horizon. Its backside seemed to touch the low black moon overhead. Beyond the mountain was a shoreline that had been rubbed out of charcoal, and beyond the shoreline was an ocean without waves, an ocean like smooth volcanic glass frozen around fiery starlight. The glass shattered into a brief mist as something breached its surface, something that might have been octopus or whale or both. Oiled and puckered flesh, shiny pink against the surrounding darkness. It rolled lazily under the boiling ozone and then slipped back into the depths, leaving behind a quiet ripple.

I had said farewell to Savin Hill, but not to the coast. What was left of my house remained by the seaside, looking out over the twisted likeness of the Atlantic. My new world was a face in a funny-house mirror. It was a grinning, howling, wounded parody of Earth. An aborted twin swimming the mad womb of another universe.

I'd fallen to my knees at the closet's threshold. Looking down, I saw no house beneath me, no walls. The office floated on empty space. My bright room was a candle flame without a candle to hold it. Leaning, I reached out into the warm, humid air and under the floor on which I sat. The floor was not there on the other side. I could stick my fingers up through the boards—that is, the horizontal plane where the boards *should* have been—but I could not poke myself or even see those fingers. The part of me inside the office and the part of me outside the office belonged to two different places . . . and those places couldn't have been further apart. I waved a slow hello to the world. If something had been looking, it would have seen my hand and nothing else.

And then something was.

The mountain by the shore opened a pair of yellow searchlight eyes. One shaggy batwing ear perked up atop its head. I pulled my hand back into the closet, but it was too late. I'd been spotted. The mountain rose to staggering heights. It had four legs and four paws, each as large as a Victorian house. Its body was thin for its size, nothing but flesh and bone and fur. Its tail swept at the stars like an eager broom.

My hungry friend.

He remembered me.

He came across the wasteland in a prancing run, moving over the ravines as if they were cracks in a sidewalk. I could hear his booming steps, could see them splitting the ground and shaking the world, but I could not feel them from the office. Roses flattened in the wind made by his passing, and then he was here; in a skip and a bound, he had cleared the gulf between the shoreline and my floating cell. From then on I saw only the small, close piece of him that fit in my window frame.

His fur was not crawling with spiders. It *was* spiders: the scrabbling limbs and bodies of tarantulas. They clothed him, fed on him, happy parasites on a starved host. I watched their fangs dip in and out of his flesh, drawing blood like oil from parched earth. The big spiders had little spiders on them, and the little spiders had baby spiders. This right here, swarming in front of me, was the consciousness I had felt in the sky. This was the creation of Tiffany's father as seen through a microscope, and these ravenous children were her brothers and sisters, born on the blackened side of some celestial coin whose face was Earth.

Outside the window, fur gave way to drooping jowls and deep red gums. A slight breeze reached me through the doorway . . . a breeze that smelled of spoiled fish. I knew then where I had gone when I'd crawled into the closet. God help me, but I knew. I had crawled into my hungry friend's mouth. He had been lying over the ravine, just as he had been the night I followed my mother into the basement and fell into his world. He had been sleeping, and I had crawled into his *mouth*. Had he tasted me? When I dug my bare fingers into his tongue, thinking it was carpet, had he tasted me? I watched now as that same tongue fell away from the window like a damp pink curtain, revealing a cruel, jagged darkness, and I knew something else as well. Hell was not a pit of fire. Hell was a warm cavern lined with teeth, and a belly that was never full.

At last, shining, came the yellow of an eye.

Its glow flooded the office with ethereal, honeyed light. The light was as cold as ice water, and I shivered—gasped— as it poured over me, pulling my shadow to the typewriter across the room. Then the glow dimmed, and I was staring at the black of his pupil. At myself on his pupil, imprisoned like a fly in dark amber. I reached out through the doorway and touched my reflection. Felt him see me. Felt him *feel* me.

"No," I told him. "Not yet."

I pulled my hand back.

I shut the closet door.

59

My mother used to say reading takes you places but writing brings you home. I was skeptical. I'd watched her at work on a novel, and it would have been easier to reel a rocket in from outer space than drag Bev Jacoby out of her head. Now I understand that she wasn't speaking about her head. She was speaking about her heart.

To write is to find what you have lost.

When I began my story, I had no idea where it would take me. I was simply moving from sentence to sentence like someone following a trail of footprints down a dark shoreline. At first the footprints were shallow, smudged out by the waves, but as I walked they grew deeper and more defined. Along the way I passed the things I'd left behind. People, places, bobbing in the low tide or washed up on the sand like shipwrecks. I passed Lu, my receptionist, my assistant, my friend. I passed my dentist chair, that old medieval torture device, and the mouthmask I wore to hide myself from foul breath. I passed a park bench from the Boston Common and a reclining chair from the movie theater. I passed a crumpled ball of paper, a poem about sonlight, and I passed the sun, too. It paved a bright track across the water before falling over the horizon, and the stars that came out in its absence pierced the sky and made the night bleed red. I passed my father's cowboy hat, half buried and surrounded by white roses. I passed my mother's body, zipped up in a black bag with her engagement ring still on her finger. And I passed Cassie, naked and lovely, the foam off the ocean gathered on her skin like soap bubbles. Cassie, whispering that my place was with the people I cared about and the people who cared about me. Cassie, wearing the key to my house around her neck.

Last of all I passed myself.

I'd gone astray. I'd let desperation take my hand and lead me away from home. I remember the crunch of Mom's nose. The crack of her skull against the brick wall. She told me she was sorry for what she had done to me, and I am sorry for what I have done to her. But it cannot be taken back. Death cannot be taken back by anyone. Except perhaps Tiffany's father. I wonder what she did with her mother's body, how she said her goodbyes. She could not have called the police, not unless she wanted to spend some time in a locked room explaining what no one would believe. Either the old dead woman on her couch was her mom and there would have been questions, or the old dead woman on the couch wasn't her mom and there would have been questions. I wonder where she will go now with nothing to keep her in Boston. I wonder who she'll become. I hope she'll find a little peace someday. I really do.

It's becoming hard to type. The work has swollen my fingers, and so have the bites. Since I met my hungry friend in the closet, he has stayed close. His spiders slip into the office through the cracks along the baseboard. They crawl out between the keys and nibble on my fingers. I am scared to slap at them in case I misspell a word. The ream of papers ran dry a while ago. First I wrote on the back of the pages I had already used. Now I am writing on the back of my mother's poems, the ones she finished and forgot about after she tucked them away for safekeeping. There are not many poems left. One way or another, my story will soon be done.

I'm getting low on food, but it is the water that worries me. I have only one bottle now and it is half empty. The other bottles I filled with urine and dumped. I should tell you that my hungry friend is also a sleepy friend (he is host to a legion of vampires, after all). He takes regular naps over the ravine, and when he does, his mouth rests around my office. It's as if he has swallowed me . . . and in a way I suppose he has. Nothing brings me more pleasure than opening the closet door and giving my tuckered-out pal a little something to drink. Luckily for him, all this bread and peanut butter has cemented my intestines or I'd have something for him to eat, too. You'd better believe it.

My hair has collected dust from the ceiling, and my skin is a pan covered in grease. I smell like an orchard whose fruit has rotted on the branches. Occasionally I take a break to wipe myself down with the curtain. The sky outside never fails to hold my gaze. It is wonderful and terrifying. It is a stew of blood that gives life and promises death. I imagine what it would be like to float into the sky, to swim over the world with the stars cutting my back as Tiffany does in her dreams. Does her father ever fold up His wings? And if He does, if He comes down to the ground from His high cold throne . . . does He walk the land as man or beast? These thoughts haunt me more than any other. I watch for Him. I wait for Him to return, but He has not so far. His night is a rare thing, and for that I am grateful.

Sometimes I sleep. The room is plenty warm even without covers. I do not know if that means winter has broken on Earth, or if the heat of my new world is simply bleeding through the walls. It does not matter either way. I make a pillow out of my arm and lay on the floorboards with the spiders. If my dreams are bad and I toss and turn, I wake covered in bites. If I am still, they leave me alone. The last time I slept, one of the lights went out over the desk. The office is very dim now. If the other light goes out, it will be completely dark.

I have a lot to think about and only a little left to say.

I think about my mom. I miss her. I think about Shawna and the sucker I gave her to make up for nicking her gums. When I close my eyes, I can see her in the library at her school and I am comforted to know that she will be all right. I believe my mom would be glad too, knowing there's at least one young girl out there who still likes books. It is not a great consolation. It is a tiny, tiny thing next to the grief I carry, but I hold it close, for even the smallest jewel shines.

I think about Tiffany. About the tooth in her mouth and the pain we passed back and forth to one another, like a cup of poisoned wine. I made a promise to myself in her car as we drove to her apartment. I swore to remember the games she played. Pretending to be homeless. Leaving me the number for a funeral home. But I forgot. I listened to her story, and I lost sight of her hate for me along the way. Perhaps she lost sight of it as well. Yes, I think so. In telling her story, I think she let go of some of her anger. I also think she told the truth . . . at least as she knew it. Then her mother stopped breathing, and our fragile peace shattered once and for all. So what did she do? She reached one last time for that cup of poisoned wine. Because it was there. Because she had nothing else. And in that terrible vulnerable moment, I was more than willing to swallow what she gave me. I never stopped to consider that Lisa's boyfriend might have been a fabrication, that instead of disappearing from Earth he might never have existed in the first place. Think about it. *Really* think about it. If Lisa had actually had a boyfriend, Tiffany would have mentioned him—and his fate—long before our ugly farewell. She would not have held out on that valuable, tragic piece of information, not when she had already told me so much. I believe that. I do. But if my belief isn't enough, if my faith in Tiffany and the tiny human connection we found isn't enough, then consider what she said herself . . . what it took typing this for me to remember. It was just a few words. An offhand remark, easily forgotten, but key to understanding her relationship with Lisa. *We had no one else.* That's what she told me. *We had no one else.* The two young women shared a friendship built on loneliness, and a friendship like that has no room for a third person. Especially not a lover. Lisa's boyfriend was a desperate lie, a drop of poison from a blackened tooth. I had taken away Tiffany's family, and so she took away mine. With my hand, my fear, she pushed Cassie out of my life. If I hadn't been so distraught, I would have seen Tiffany's last words for what they were: a wild attempt to hurt me. To make me as alone as I had made her.

Cassie.

Cassie.

Always my thoughts return to Cassie. She is the star around which my sunless world orbits (I'm sorry, Mom. I hope you'll forgive me for writing such an awful, sentimental line on your typewriter, even if it is true). I look back at our night together. I've built a house for that night inside of me, and we live together there now. We eat Chinese around the kitchen table and make hungry, urgent love inside the bathtub and lay naked in cozy lamplight. Cassie sits on top of me in bed, holding my hand to her heart. Her key dangles from her neck, almost touching mine. And I wonder—oh, I wonder—if it was chance that the moments we shared went untainted by all the horrors of the week, or if something bigger was at play. Protecting us. Guarding us. Something that belongs to this world and this world alone, like Tiffany's tooth belongs to her father's world. Something that cannot exist there, in that place of endless night and hunger.

Tiffany said there was no way back, and she was speaking the truth. The only truth that she knew. But she was wrong. I had to write it all out to see. I had to relive the darkest moments of my nightmare to find the light that was there the whole time. My mother found me. She found me underneath the black moon of that red sky, and she showed me the way back. I wasn't with her in the basement, we were lost in our separate worlds, but she found me all the same. With her hand around mine, moss thinned to concrete . . . stairs built themselves up where there had been no stairs before . . . and the door that had shut behind me, the door that had locked itself and thrown away the key, opened once again.

Don't you see? Tiffany never had a home. She never had a home, and the people she sent away—her first foster father, her wayward friend—they had nowhere to go back to. No *one* to go back to or to bring them back.

But I do.

So I wait. I hold the key around my throat, and I wait for Cassie to come. She will. I know she will, and when she does, I will take her hand and follow her through the office door. Out into the open air. Out over the wasteland where my hungry friend wanders beneath the stars. I will follow her down the hall that is no longer there, and I will feel the carpet that is beneath our feet, even if I do not see it. Then I *will* see it. And then the stairs beyond. And together we will walk out into the daylight and shut the door on this sunless, loveless world.

Together.

That is the way home.

Roses are red
Violets are blue
My name is Bev
Who are you?

Roses are red
Violets are blue
It's snowing outside

Roses are red
Violets are blue
Sugar is sweet
And so is Hugh
Jackman

Roses are red
Violets are blue
I'm drinking coffee
HA HA HA!
Don't tell, okay?

Roses are red
Violets are bule

Roses are red
Violets are blue
You were lost
And I found you

I write this quickly. In the dark. The second light in the office went out some time ago, but my fingers know where to move. The spiders are very bad now. They cover my hands as they cover the body of my hungry friend outside the office. I feel him panting through the cracks in the walls. His breath is a wind in the room. It throws the empty shopping bags all about and makes a great deal of noise, and yet, just a moment ago, I heard another sound. A tiny, tiny, far-off sound, but to me the loudest sound I have ever heard.

I heard a key turning inside a lock.

AUTHOR'S NOTE

You're here. You've finished, or you've skipped to the end looking for a photo of me with my hand stroking my beard. In which case you're out of luck, because like my beard, no such thing exists. Whatever brought you to this page, you took a gamble first. You opened My Hungry Friend and gave a little of your life to it.

Thank you.

If you'd be willing to sacrifice a few more moments by writing a brief, honest review on Amazon, I'd greatly appreciate it. Reviews help a book find its audience. Without them, the seats down there stay empty. So throw that tomato, clap those hands, shout, scream, flail, break dance in the aisles or set the building on fire, just make some noise. And get out before the cops come.

See you next time around, I hope.

Until then, love letters and death threats can be directed to dbhfiction@gmail.com.

96845829R00117